**She'd vowed never to get involved with a client. Not to trust any man.**

Except…how could she resist this sexy, strong man who would give his life for a little boy?

"How about you?" she asked softly.

Cash's eyes darkened with pain, then flickered with something akin to desire. "I'll be all right when we find Tyler."

An image of her own son, pale and lifeless, taunted her. BJ looked down, battling tears. "Me, too. I just hope and pray…" She let the sentence trail off, unable to voice her worst fears out loud.

"Hey," Cash murmured. "Don't give up. I'm not."

He was talking about Tyler. And she hadn't given up on finding him.

But there was no bringing back her son. It was too late.

The grief she'd lived with since she'd lost him welled up and threatened to bring her to her knees again.

She looked up into Cash's eyes and was moved by his tenderness. Desperate for his touch, for comfort, she pressed her hand over his chest. His heart pounded, strong and alive, beneath her palm.

She leaned into him, and he brushed her hair from her cheek. "BJ?"

"Shh, just hold me for a minute."

He made a low sound in his throat as if he was struggling not to touch her. Then his eyes darkened, and he pulled her up against him.

# The Missing McCullen

## RITA HERRON

This is a work of fiction. Names, characters, places, locations and incidents are purely fictional and bear no relationship to any real life individuals, living or dead, or to any actual places, business establishments, locations, events or incidents. Any resemblance is entirely coincidental.



First Published in Great Britain 2017
By Mills & Boon, an imprint of HarperCollins*Publishers*
1 London Bridge Street, London, SE1 9GF

Large Print edition 2017



ISBN: 978-0-263-07230-3

Our policy is to use papers that are natural, renewable and recyclable products and made from wood grown in sustainable forests. The logging and manufacturing processes conform to the legal environmental regulations of the country of origin.

Printed and bound in Great Britain
by CPI Antony Rowe, Chippenham, Wiltshire

*USA TODAY* bestselling author **Rita Herron** wrote her first book when she was twelve but didn't think real people grew up to be writers. Now she writes so she doesn't have to get a real job. A former kindergarten teacher and workshop leader, she traded storytelling for writing romance, and now she writes romantic comedies and romantic suspense. Rita lives in Georgia with her family. She loves to hear from readers, so please visit her website, www.ritaherron.com.

# *Prologue*

Ray McCullen faced his brothers, Maddox and Brett, with a knot in his stomach. For months they'd been searching for twin brothers who'd been kidnapped from their parents at birth.

They would be thirty this month.

He had good news and bad news. "I found one of the twins."

Maddox balled his hands into fists. "You don't sound happy about it."

"Where is he?" Brett asked.

"The babies were left at a church about an hour from Pistol Whip. Apparently, one of them was adopted, but the other was sickly and wound up being placed in foster care. A nurse took him in for a while, and named him Cash Koker."

"Where is he now?" Maddox asked.

Ray turned to the whiteboard where they'd listed clues regarding the boys' whereabouts. He tacked a photo on the board.

"I used age progression software and a special program I have to locate doppelgangers. This is him."

Maddox studied the photo. "He looks like a McCullen. Same stubborn jaw. Dark hair."

"He's got your high forehead and dark eyes, Maddox," Brett said.

Maddox cleared his throat. "The DNA matched?"

Ray nodded. "Yeah, his was in the system, but I still want another test done for verification."

"I agree," Maddox said.

"Does he know about us?" Brett asked.

"I don't think so."

Maddox crossed his arms. "You said his DNA was in the system. Does that mean what I think it means?"

Ray gave a quick nod. "He has a record. Got

into some trouble as a juvenile, then a couple of bar brawls in his twenties."

"Hell, so did I. Is that it?" Brett asked.

Ray grunted. "Afraid not." He tacked another photo on the board. This picture was a mug shot. "Our long-lost brother has just been arrested for murder."

# *Chapter One*

"I didn't kill anyone." Cash Koker flexed his hands on the scarred wooden table of the interrogation room, barely resisting the urge to punch Sheriff Jim Jasper in the jaw.

He'd answered these damn questions a dozen times already, but for some reason, the bastard thought he could browbeat Cash into admitting to murder.

There was no way in hell he'd confess to a crime he hadn't committed.

The bloodstains beneath his fingernails mocked him. Blood that belonged to Sondra, the woman he allegedly had killed.

"Just look at her picture," Sheriff Jasper said.

"She was young and beautiful, but you took her life away from her."

Cash swallowed hard as he glanced at the image. Sondra was twenty-two, with pale skin and blond hair that fell to her shoulders.

That hair was tangled and bloody in the photograph. Her throat had been cut, her eyes wide in shock and horror. Blood soaked her thin white blouse, and her hands, which she'd obviously used to fight her attacker.

"I didn't kill her," Cash said again. "I cared about Sondra. We were friends."

"Friends?" Sheriff Jasper crossed his beefy arms and leaned back in his chair. Although he was only a few years older than Cash, the cocky man thought he owned the town. He also got around. Apparently women thought he was attractive.

Cash didn't like anything about him.

"Sondra's daddy said there was a lot more to it than friendship," Jasper said snidely.

Cash chewed the inside of his cheek. Mr. Elmore was a paranoid, pompous, demanding jerk who was rich as sin but barely paid his ranch hands minimum wage. He couldn't keep help because he was cheap and damn difficult to work for.

"In fact, Elmore claims that you knocked up his daughter, and that you denied paternity. He says you slit Sondra's throat to keep her from filing for child support."

Cash thumped his boot on the floor. "He's wrong. I'm not the little boy's father. You know as well as I do that a DNA test can prove it." Although, he had grown attached to the spunky three-year-old.

"Then who is the father?"

Cash sighed. "I don't know. Sondra never told me."

Jasper grabbed him by his shirt collar and practically yanked Cash across the table. "Listen to me, you good-for-nothing piece of trash. Lester Elmore is a respected rancher around here. He doesn't lie." He shoved another picture in front of Cash's face. "Neither does the evidence. We've got Sondra's blood under your nails, and a video cam clip from last night showing you entering the motel where she died."

Cash shifted, his mind racing for answers. The last thing he remembered was meeting her at the bar, because she'd been upset. He'd had a drink and they'd walked outside.

The rest of the night was a damn blank.

Hours later, he'd woken up in a motel room beside Sondra's dead body. He'd been in shock, panicked, and had called an ambulance. He'd also called Sondra's father.

It hadn't occurred to him that the man would accuse him of murder.

"You could ease your conscience by telling me what happened," the sheriff growled. "Or let me guess—you had a lover's quarrel, and she threatened to cut you out of the kid's life. Am I getting close?"

Cash went stone still. Nothing he could say would convince this man that he was innocent.

Worse, the evidence was damning. Given it, and the fact that Elmore owned half the town, they could lock him away and he'd never see the light of day again.

"You are way off base," Cash said matter-of-factly. "I told you—we weren't lovers." In fact, he would never have gone to a motel with Sondra. They didn't have that kind of relationship. "Why aren't you looking at Elmore? He probably had enemies."

"Elmore is not the problem," Sheriff Jasper snapped.

"But I didn't do anything," Cash's mind raced. "You should be looking for someone else with a motive. Sondra said some guy named Ronnie was bothering her."

Sheriff Jasper raised a brow. "Stop trying to put the blame on someone else, and tell me what you did with Tyler. If Elmore gets his grandson back, he might go easier on you."

Cash's pulse jumped. "What the hell are you talking about? You don't know where Tyler is?"

The sheriff shoved him backward so hard the chair legs clacked on the floor. "Don't act dumb,

Koker. If you took that kid, you're going down for kidnapping and murder."

Panic streaked through Cash. Someone had kidnapped Tyler?

*Three days later*

BJ ALEXANDER HAD made a lot of mistakes in her short career as an attorney. She just hoped coming to Cash Koker's defense wasn't one of them.

But her father and Joe McCullen had been friends, and now that Joe was dead, her father had asked her to help his sons find out more about their long-lost brother.

*Possible long-lost brother*, she amended.

She slipped from the safety of her small sedan, letting the warmth of the summer day chase away the chill inside her as she studied the sheriff's office.

The building was a one-story, ancient brick structure with mud caking the brick. She'd called ahead and Sheriff Jasper had filled her in on the arrest.

Cash Koker had been locked up for murdering a young woman named Sondra Elmore. Apparently, Cash had once worked for Sondra's father on the Wagon Wheel Ranch.

Cash insisted he was innocent.

Like she hadn't heard that before.

A year ago, she'd represented a man named Davis Turner, who claimed he'd been framed for murder. After losing her ex-husband and son, she'd been in a bad place. Vulnerable.

Davis was charming, convincing, and seemed compassionate. She'd broken the cardinal rule of not getting involved with a client and had allowed their relationship to become personal.

She had gotten him acquitted in record time.

Two days later, she realized he'd played her. She'd overheard him talking to his mistress on the phone. He'd admitted he was guilty.

Worse, he was a free man because of her, and he couldn't be retried for killing his wife.

She'd hated herself for being so naive. Hated that she may have put another person in danger by helping a killer walk.

She wouldn't make that mistake with this case. *If* she took it.

Despite her father and Joe McCullen's friendship, that was a big if.

Cash Koker had to convince her he was innocent.

Resolved, she opened the door to the sheriff's office and entered. A tiny older woman with gray hair sat at a reception desk. Her name tag read Imogene.

BJ identified herself. "I'm here to meet with Cash Koker."

A tough-looking man in a sheriff's uniform, probably in his midthirties, appeared in the doorway. He might have been handsome if his scowl wasn't so off-putting.

He hitched his thumb toward the back. "You the attorney gonna represent that scumbag in there?"

BJ stiffened. It sounded as if the sheriff had already convicted Cash.

Did he have concrete evidence proving Cash was guilty?

CASH HAD TO get out of this cell.

He'd been here all weekend, shut off as if he was one of the most wanted people in Wyoming.

Dammit. He hated to be confined. Small spaces triggered bad memories of being locked in the closet when he was a kid in foster care.

He lurched up from the cot and paced the cell. He'd racked his brain all weekend, struggling to piece together what had happened Friday night. Had someone drugged him?

Was he with Sondra when she was murdered? How did he end up in a motel with her?

And what about Tyler? Where was that precious little guy?

Panic seized him at the scenarios that flashed through his head. He'd had his share of bad knocks in foster care and knew the dark side of the human mind. Knew the depravity that existed, and how difficult it was for a little kid to defend himself against those bigger than him.

He bit the inside of his cheek, battling despair. Maybe the sheriff had it wrong. Sondra had been upset when she'd called him to meet her. She could have dropped Tyler with a friend for safe-keeping.

If so, wouldn't that person have come forward when news of her murder was revealed? Surely Elmore and the sheriff had posted an Amber Alert by now and had people searching.

If Sondra's killer had kidnapped Tyler, though, there was no telling what he'd do to the little boy.

Elmore had money. He'd probably made enemies. If someone wanted to get back at him, killing Sondra and kidnapping her child was the way to do it.

Cash dropped onto the cot and lowered his head into his hands. He'd called the lawyer in town, but got the message machine. So far no one had shown up.

Hell, for all he knew the man was in Elmore's pocket.

The door connecting the sheriff's front office and the cells screeched open. Cash braced himself for another interrogation.

The sheriff stomped toward him, but he wasn't alone this time.

A young woman with hair as black as coal and skin like ivory followed him. Cash couldn't help himself—his gaze swept over her, from those sexy black stilettos, to the curves hidden beneath her stuffy suit, to the wary look in her startling green eyes.

His body instantly hardened. After all, he was a man. And any man would appreciate her femininity.

Although whatever reason she was here, she didn't look happy about it.

He lurched up from the cot and raked a hand through his hair, well aware he looked scruffy and hadn't showered in days. Even though he'd washed his hands, the scent of Sondra's blood still lingered on his skin, and he wore drab prison clothes.

Jasper's boots shuffled on the concrete as he approached. When he reached Cash's cell, he halted, keys jangling in his beefy hand. The woman stood beside him, her dainty chin lifted high as if she was assessing Cash.

"Koker, this woman claims she's your lawyer."

Sheriff Jasper looked at him as if Cash was an animal who needed to be put down, not have representation.

He narrowed his eyes. "My lawyer?"

The woman cleared her throat. "Mr. Patton had a stroke. My name is BJ Alexander."

Damn, her husky voice made Cash's body tighten even more.

"Sheriff Jasper, I need to talk to my client in private," she said. "Open the cell, please."

Jasper scowled at her, but jammed the key in the cell door and opened it. For a brief second, something akin to fear flickered in the woman's eyes.

She might be tough, but she was afraid of Cash.

That didn't sit well in his gut.

He would never lay a hand on a woman, at least not in violence.

But that damn sheriff had probably already convinced her he was guilty.

BJ SCRUTINIZED CASH. The man looked rough. Hair a little too long. Eyes deep, dark. Distrustful.

Body…well, hell, he was built. Broad shoulders. Tall. Muscles everywhere.

Which meant he was strong enough to overpower a woman.

The McCullens had just learned they had two brothers who'd been kidnapped at birth. They thought Cash was one of them.

Since she'd spoken to them, she'd done her research.

Cash had grown up in the foster care system. At twelve he'd been placed in a ranch home for troubled boys. He'd learned ranching skills, and as an adult had worked on several spreads across Wyoming. He'd moved half a dozen times, though, which made her wonder if he was searching for something, or if he'd been asked to leave.

The head of the ranch for boys had described him as sullen, brooding, angry. Said he needed guidance from a strong male.

Guidance he'd never received.

Two of his employers claimed he was an excellent rider, a natural cattleman and that he'd kept to himself but done a good job. After a season or two, he'd left of his own accord, saying it was time for him to move on.

He was a drifter. Probably had a new woman in every county he moved to.

All the more reason she should maintain her professional demeanor. She wouldn't fall prey to his charms like she had with Davis.

Although at the moment, Cash looked beaten—not like a womanizer. The disdain in his eyes was palpable.

"Sheriff, please show Mr. Koker to an interrogation room so we can talk." At least they would both be more comfortable. Sitting on that tiny cot beside Cash Koker was not an option. Sex appeal radiated from him in waves. There was also an air of danger about him that put her on edge.

The sheriff grunted in compliance, then gestured for Cash to hold out his hands so he could cuff them.

A muscle ticked in Cash's jaw, but he did as the man ordered. Jasper led him to a small room with a plain wooden table and two chairs. Cash's expression was grim as he sank into the chair.

Handcuffs clanged as he spread his fingers on the table. Calluses and scars marked his hands and arms, a telltale sign that he did manual labor.

The sheriff cleared his throat. “You want me to stay?”

BJ shook her head. She couldn’t show fear or any emotion. “No, I’m fine.”

Jasper worked his mouth from side to side, one hand on his holster. “Yell if you need me.” He squeezed Cash’s shoulder so hard the prisoner’s jaw tightened. “Touch her and you’ll be sorry.”

A frisson of nerves prickled BJ’s spine as the sheriff left the room and Cash turned his rage toward her.

A jagged scar curled beneath his hairline on the right side, making him look frightening and sexy at the same time. She envisioned him riding a bull or galloping across rugged terrain, and her heart stuttered.

She gripped the edge of the table, silently cursing herself. She could not allow herself to think of him as attractive.

"All right, lady," he said gruffly. "What are you doing here?"

BJ forced herself to remember that he had no clue he was a McCullen. She'd expected the McCullen men would want to meet him, but they'd had trouble with a half brother named Bobby, and were cautious.

After all, Horseshoe Creek Ranch belonged to all of Joe McCullen's sons, which meant that Maddox, Brett and Ray would have to share land with the lost twins.

They intended to find the truth about Cash's character *before* they disclosed their relationship.

"I came to decide if I want to represent you," BJ said. "To do that, I need to hear your version of what happened the night Sondra Elmore died."

He arched a thick brow. "Why? You gonna believe me?"

BJ leaned forward, snagging his gaze with a cold look. "Sarcasm is not your friend right now, Mr. Koker. The truth might be, though, if you want to tell it."

Shoulders squared, she gathered the file, ready

to leave. The last thing she intended to do was work for some ungrateful jerk who didn't want her help. "If not, I'll leave you alone and you can rot in that cell."

# *Chapter Two*

BJ folded her arms across her chest. "You have ten seconds to decide how this will go before I walk out that door."

Anger flashed across Cash's face, along with distrust—and the realization that he did need help. That he might have to suck it up if he wanted to fight these charges.

"Just sit down," he growled.

BJ shook her head. "I don't take orders from you, Mr. Koker. If I accept your case, I expect respect. But first, you have to convince me that you're innocent."

Tension rippled between them. He shifted and

stared at his fingers again, obviously torn. Or was he trying to concoct a convincing lie?

"All right, Miss Alexander," he said. "Please sit back down."

A tiny smile of victory twitched at her mouth, but she masked it, maintaining her neutral expression. He had said please, though, so she slipped into the chair facing him.

"Now tell me—has Tyler been found? Is he okay?"

"I'm afraid there hasn't been any word on the boy," she said quietly.

Cash pressed his knuckles over his eyes. "You have to find him."

"Do you know where he is?" she asked in a tight voice.

"No." His gaze met hers, suspicion flaring. "Are you working for Elmore?"

BJ frowned. "Why would you ask that?"

"Because Lester Elmore never thought I was good enough for his daughter." A muscle ticked in his jaw. "Did he pay you to get dirt on me so he could railroad me to prison for killing his daughter?"

BJ locked stubborn gazes with him. "For the record, I've never met the man, and he didn't pay me to do anything." She let that sentence sink in for a brief second. "In fact, I can't be bought by anyone, so even if he had offered, I would have turned him down."

"Really?" Koker's mouth curled in a sardonic grin. "You mean I'm looking at a real-life *honest* lawyer?"

She gave him a flat look. "Believe it or not, yes."

She removed photos of the crime scene and spread them across the table. Cash zeroed in on a shot of Sondra Elmore drenched in blood, and his face paled.

"Did you kill Sondra?" BJ asked.

A tortured look darkened his eyes. "No."

BJ waited, hoping he'd elaborate, but he didn't.

She tapped a picture of a bloody hunting knife the sheriff had found at the scene. "This isn't your knife?"

Cash cursed. "Yes, it is, but I didn't kill Sondra with it."

"Then why was it lying on the floor beside her?"

"I have no idea." He leaned his head on his hands and inhaled several deep breaths. "Think about it. If I had killed her, you think I'd be dumb enough to leave a weapon behind with my fingerprints on it?"

No. But she had to ask.

Still, this man was a stranger to her. She wasn't certain she could trust her instincts, either, not after the mess she'd made with Davis.

THE PICTURE OF Sondra covered in blood made Cash's stomach roil.

The lawyer cleared her throat. "You knew Sondra well, didn't you, Cash? You were friendly?"

He gave her a scathing look. "We were friends. Period."

"According to the sheriff's notes and his interview with Mr. Elmore, you were more than that."

Cash shook his head. "Not true."

"You weren't lovers?" she asked bluntly.

Cash shifted. "I answered that already. We were just friends."

"They why did her father think you two were involved?"

He made a low sound in his throat. "Sondra may have implied that we were."

The lawyer tapped her manicured nails on the table. A reminder that his were ragged and had been bloodstained, that the cops had forensics that would work against him.

Even though he'd washed them, in his mind's eye, he could still see Sondra's blood.

"I see," she said wryly. "And you allowed her father to believe a lie?"

"I didn't like it. I told her that." Cash shrugged. "But I didn't dispute it."

"You two argued about the issue?"

"Not really. She begged me not to say anything and I agreed."

Cash rolled his fingers into fists. If he admitted that he and Sondra had argued the afternoon she died, he'd give this lawyer a motive.

"Why did Sondra allow her father to believe you were the boy's father? And why would you let her do that?"

"Elmore's a paranoid jerk who warned all of his employees, including me, to keep their hands off of his daughter. He wanted to keep her in some kind of bubble, but she was rebellious."

The woman raised a brow. "Rebellious as in she dated the hands to make him angry?"

"Sometimes."

"If she was so rebellious, why didn't she just move out?"

Cash shrugged. "First of all, Elmore controlled her trust fund. But I think she was secretly hoping her father would come around and accept Tyler."

"She dated you to get back at her father?"

"I told you, we never dated," he said firmly. "She was too young for me."

"But she got pregnant and told Elmore you were the father."

Cash heaved a weary breath. God, she was

a professional interrogator. "Yes. But the boy wasn't mine. Do the DNA test and you'll see."

"We'll get to that." She glanced at her file, then back up at him. "So who was the child's father?"

He wished to hell he knew. "She never told me."

"Why not? You said you were close."

"I don't know why. She just didn't want to talk about him." Cash tensed. He was painting himself into a corner.

"Tell me more about your relationship then."

"She was like a kid sister to me," he said. "She used to come out to the barn and yammer on like a teenager. Mostly venting about her father and how overprotective he was. He pressured her to give up the baby after it was born so she wouldn't shame the family."

"But she kept the child?"

"Yeah, she was tenderhearted. Loved animals and kids." She'd cried on his shoulder about that decision. Cash had promised to provide emotional support if she kept the child and raised it on her own.

Yet he'd let her down and she was dead.

"Elmore allowed you to stay on after Tyler was born?"

Cash gritted his teeth. "No, he fired me, then bad-mouthed me to other ranchers. Finally, I found a job on a small spread not too far away."

"You still saw Sondra and Tyler?"

"Mostly Tyler. Sometimes she dropped him off so we could spend time together. Said he needed a male role model." Cash had been surprised she'd chosen him for the job. But hey, the kid didn't have a daddy and Cash related to that.

Images of the little boy tagging along behind him taunted Cash. Tyler loved horses and riding. He constantly talked about joining the rodeo.

"Cash?"

BJ's soft voice dragged him from the memories. God, what if something had happened to Tyler? "Tyler's three now. He's a pistol."

"Do you think Sondra intentionally got pregnant? Maybe she thought this man would marry her if they had a child."

"Sondra wouldn't have done that."

Disbelief tinged the lawyer's eyes. "Did she tell the father about the baby?"

Cash nodded. "He didn't want anything to do with Tyler."

"So Sondra never revealed the boy's father's name?"

"I told you she didn't," he said, his irritation mounting.

She fell silent for a moment. "If you didn't kill Sondra, it's possible that this other man did. Was Sondra afraid of him?"

Cash scrubbed his hand over his chin. "I don't know. Maybe."

"Tell me about the night she died," BJ said.

He'd been struggling to recall Friday evening, but the entire night was a fog. "She was upset when she called me, but she didn't explain. I assumed she and her daddy had had an argument, but I guess she could have fought with Tyler's father."

BJ pursed her lips. "She must have had a good reason to keep his identity a secret. He could be married or a prominent figure in the community.

He had something to lose if word leaked he had a child."

"That's what I figured." Cash's heart hammered. The only way to clear himself was to find Sondra's killer. "What if she'd decided to come clean about him? Or maybe she needed money or help."

"Makes sense. If he didn't want his identity exposed, he could have killed her to keep her quiet." BJ crossed her legs, drawing his attention to their long slender shape. She must have noticed, because a second later she uncrossed them and leaned forward. "We need to know his name."

"If I knew his name, trust me, I'd tell you." Fear made his throat thick. "If your theory is right and he didn't want the boy, he could have killed him."

Her frown deepened. "It would be pretty cold-hearted to kill a child."

Cash nodded. He couldn't allow himself to even think about losing Tyler. But he didn't want to go to prison for a crime he hadn't committed. Offering another suspect could help his case.

"I'll try to get ahold of Tyler's birth certificate," she suggested.

Cash nodded again. "Look into Elmore, too. Maybe someone had a grudge against him and kidnapped Tyler for blackmail money."

BJ cleared her throat. "True."

"I tried to tell Sheriff Jasper this, but he didn't believe me." Cash didn't like any of the scenarios that flashed through his mind. "A few of the ranchers had squabbles with him, but I don't think they'd resort to kidnapping."

"I'll ask around," BJ agreed.

"Has Elmore received a ransom call?" Cash asked.

She shook her head. "Not that I know of, but I'll talk to him."

Emotions thickened his throat as he pictured the times he'd played horseshoe with the little guy. Then another time when Tyler had climbed a tree, but was too afraid to climb down, so Cash had rescued him.

That little boy had dug a hole in Cash's heart. They had to find him and make sure he was safe.

BJ TAPPED HER fingernails on the table again. “There’s another possibility, Cash. Do you have any enemies? Someone who would frame you for murder?”

Turmoil hardened Cash’s face. “Elmore disliked me, but I haven’t seen him in a while. Other than him, I can’t think of anyone.”

BJ’s lungs squeezed. She’d come here skeptical about this man’s innocence. But he couldn’t fake the fear in his eyes or voice—he was sincerely worried about that child.

Still, she had to remain objective and consider every possibility.

“The sheriff thinks that you took Tyler and planned to blackmail Elmore.”

“That’s ridiculous. Besides, I didn’t have to kill anyone to execute that plan, if that was really my intent.”

“You must have hated him for firing you and blackballing you. You could use the money to buy your own place.”

“I did want my own spread, I’ll admit that.” Anger sizzled in his eyes. “But not bad enough to hurt Sondra. I know what it's like to grow up without a family. I loved Tyler and would never have taken his mama away."

The pain in his voice was too raw to not be real.

"Tell me what happened then," BJ said. "How did you wind up in that motel room with Sondra's blood all over you?"

He released a frustrated sigh. "Like I told you, she called me, upset, and I met her at the tavern." He rubbed his chin. "I got there and ordered a drink. She came and...we walked outside for a minute. Then everything goes blank."

"Someone knocked you out?"

"I don't know." Confusion clouded his eyes. "Either that or I was drugged."

An excuse or the truth? "Unfortunately, it's too late to test your blood for drugs."

"I realize that, but it's the only explanation I can think of." His expression turned grim. "Seriously, one minute I was talking to her, the next I woke up in the room with Sondra, and she was dead."

BJ studied him. Shock and sorrow radiated

from his eyes. If he was a liar, he was a damn good one.

But the security camera had captured his face outside that motel room. "You woke up and found her, then what?"

He lifted his shoulders in a defeated shrug. "I called 911, and then I phoned Sondra's father. I… thought I was doing the right thing."

He had done the right thing. That is, if he hadn't sliced Sondra's throat.

But BJ couldn't imagine him killing a woman in cold blood.

Maybe a crime of passion?

She needed to question the ranch hands and find out if Cash was violent. If they thought he'd had an affair with Sondra.

If he wanted to get back at Elmore.

Another possibility hit her, one she didn't want to consider. But one the DA definitely would.

What if Cash was in love with Sondra, and wanted to marry her and adopt Tyler? She could have met with him to tell him to leave her alone. Maybe she'd even fallen for another man and planned to cut Cash out of the boy's life. He could have flown into a jealous rage.

Indecision warred with the instinct that Cash was telling the truth and needed help. That either Cash or Elmore had enemies.

That one of those enemies had killed Sondra and kidnapped Tyler to get revenge.

But what had they done with Tyler?

CASH COULD SEE the wheels turning in the lawyer's head. She was trying to decide whether he was innocent or guilty.

He wasn't sure which way she was leaning.

"Miss Alexander, even if you decide not to represent me, please make sure the police search for Tyler. If Jasper thinks I did something with him, he may be dragging his feet, thinking I'll confess. Tyler could be in danger."

"I'm sure he's doing everything he can to find him," she said. "An Amber Alert has been issued and NCMEC, the National Center for Missing and Exploited Children, has been notified."

Cash still didn't trust Jasper.

An image of the precocious three-year-old teased his mind. Tyler liked to trail ride with him. He could feel the little boy's arms locked around his waist, hear him giggling when the horse broke into a canter.

He even had a Western shirt like one of Cash's and wore it when they were together.

Miss Alexander gathered the photos of Sondra and stuffed them in her briefcase. She stood, her posture rigid, her lips pressed into a thin line.

"Don't take Jasper's word for it." Cash touched her arm.

She went stone still and stared at his fingers as if he'd burned her. He released her abruptly.

Just like Elmore, she'd put him in his place with a condescending look.

Hell, he'd never be good enough for a man like Elmore or a woman like her.

It didn't matter, though. All that mattered was making sure little Tyler was safe.

"Please," he said in a gruff voice. "Find Tyler. He needs your help more than I do."

Her gaze locked with his, and he swallowed

hard. He could lose himself in those damn beautiful eyes.

But those eyes were cold and serious, assessing.

"Don't worry. I'll alert authorities to look for Tyler," she said, her voice cracking slightly. "We're meeting with the judge in an hour for a bail hearing."

Hope and despair crawled through Cash. He badly wanted out of this jail. But he was broke. All he had was a little bit of savings for the ranch he'd been dreaming about.

He was determined to have his own spread someday. Then he'd never have to bow down to bigwig ranchers like Elmore again.

"I appreciate you coming," he said, biting back his pride. "But I can't make bail."

She angled her head to look at him, her mouth forming a thin line. "Your bail money and my fee have been taken care of."

Without another word, she left, and closed the door behind her.

Cash's heart hammered as the lock clicked into

place. Who the hell had paid her? And who was posting his bail?

His ranch hand buddies didn't have money. And he didn't have family to turn to.

He refused to take charity, too.

But what choice did he have? He needed to find out who'd set him up. He sure as hell couldn't do that from the inside of a cell.

And he trusted her a hell of a lot more than he would some court appointed attorney who might know Elmore or be in his pocket.

BJ LEFT CASH with unanswered questions. The sheriff frowned at her, but stepped into the room to escort Cash to the cell.

She needed to speak to Maddox before she revealed Cash's connection to the McCullens.

The pain in his eyes ripped at her. She was still straddling the fence about his innocence or guilt, although she was leaning on the innocent side.

One thing she knew for sure, though. He loved that little boy.

And he was seriously worried about him.

Which roused her own fear for Tyler.

She rushed into the restroom, grabbed a paper towel and wetted it just as the first wave of dizziness assaulted her.

Three-year-old Tyler Elmore was missing.

She'd had no idea when she took the case. All she was told was that Cash Koker had been arrested for murder.

Panic gnawed at her as she recalled Cash's last words. He wanted her to look for the little boy. He'd chosen that over his own release.

Even though he'd denied being the child's father, he was frightened for him.

Tears blurred her eyes, and she removed the rainbow drawing she kept with her. Her son had been obsessed with rainbows and had made this one for her for Mother's Day.

Time faded and she was back with her son.

*"Mommy, tuck me in."*

*She wiped her hands on the dish towel, then went to Aaron's room. He was in his cartoon pj's, snuggled with his stuffed lion, holding his favorite book. She crawled on the bed and he nuzzled up against her as she began to read.*

*Seconds later, he fell asleep on her arm.*

*Two days later—the call that had shattered her heart. A highway patrol officer.*

*Her ex had taken Aaron on a camping trip, but they'd had a terrible accident.*

*Neither one of them had survived.*

BJ wiped the tears from her eyes, folded the drawing and put it back in her pocket. It hurt too much to think about Aaron's little innocent face looking up at her as if she'd protect him from the world, when she'd failed.

If Tyler was in danger, she had to help.

She left the bathroom, then walked up front to talk to Sheriff Jasper. "Has Mr. Elmore located his grandson?"

A vein throbbed in the lawman's neck. "No, all the more reason you tell us what that Koker guy did with Tyler."

BJ bit the inside of her cheek. The sheriff definitely had made up his mind about Cash. He'd probably lynch him if he didn't think he'd get caught.

"My conversation with my client is confidential, although I don't believe he took the child or knows where he is. He seems genuinely concerned. If you haven't followed up on the Amber Alert, do so immediately."

"I know how to do my job." Jasper's sarcastic tone implied she didn't. "You just need to push Koker to talk."

Anger mushroomed inside BJ. "I told you he didn't take the boy. Have you spoken with Mr. Elmore to see if he received a ransom call?"

"He hasn't."

BJ tensed. That wasn't a good sign. "For a moment, let's just say I'm right, Sheriff. The first forty-eight hours are critical for a missing child case." She tapped her watch. "Every minute counts. So while you're sitting here on your butt, whoever abducted Tyler is getting farther and farther away."

Which meant they might not get the little boy back alive.

That terrified her more than anything.

# *Chapter Three*

BJ stopped at the diner in town and ordered coffee and a muffin. Her stomach was too knotted to eat much, but she needed something before Cash's bail hearing.

She ran a search on her computer and found articles about Lester Elmore and his ranch, along with a story on his success. A photo of Sondra accompanying her father to a state fund-raiser when she was seventeen revealed the depth of the young woman's beauty. Her father was looking at her in adoration.

Her Facebook page revealed a photo of Sondra and Tyler. The kid had sandy-brown hair, was freckle-faced and so adorable that tears pricked her eyes. “Where are you, little guy?”

She quickly searched Sondra’s friends and posts, hoping to find a clue as to someone Sondra may have left the boy with but came up empty. Although she had a close girlfriend named Diane who’d ridden with her when Sondra had been into showing horses. Those posts were dated two years before though.

She punched in Sheriff Maddox McCullen’s phone number, sipping her coffee while she waited. The phone rang three times, then a male voice answered. “Sheriff McCullen speaking.”

“Sheriff, it’s BJ Alexander.”

A heartbeat passed. “Call me Maddox. You met Cash Koker?”

“I did,” BJ said.

“What do you think?” Maddox asked.

BJ hesitated. “I don’t think he has a clue that he has brothers or any family.”

Maddox heaved a sigh. “I figured as much. If he did, he would have probably called or shown up at Horseshoe Creek.”

Cash didn't strike her as the type to ask for handouts. "The bail hearing is soon." BJ fidgeted. "Have you read the sheriff's report?"

"No, but when I spoke to Sheriff Jasper, he was adamant that he had the right man."

"He's made up his mind," BJ said. "I don't think he's even considered that Cash might be innocent."

"So he's not investigating or looking for another suspect?" Maddox said with disgust.

"No."

"Do you think Cash is guilty?" Maddox asked.

BJ stared into her coffee, willing an answer to come to her. "I'm not sure," she said honestly. "He claims that he cared about Sondra, but denies that they were lovers. Sondra had a three-year-old little boy. That child is missing."

Maddox murmured something beneath his breath. "The sheriff thinks Cash did something with the kid?"

"Yes, but I don't."

Maddox's gruff voice jerked her from her thoughts. "What did Cash say about the boy?"

BJ massaged her temple where a headache pulsed. Kids were her soft spot. Sometimes she missed her own son so badly she could hardly breathe.

"Finding Tyler seems more important to Cash than his own defense."

"Hmm. Interesting." Maddox paused. "Who is the boy's father?"

"He claims he doesn't know." BJ sighed and recounted her conversation with Cash. Maddox was paying her, but she still had to be careful with client/attorney privilege.

"So Cash is either lying or someone drugged him and framed him," Maddox said matter-of-factly.

"Exactly."

Only to clear him, she'd have to prove it.

"Ray's still looking for the other twin. I'll have the DNA tests run on Cash and compare them to Tyler's. And I'll dig up what I can find on the Elmore family," Maddox offered. "Then I'll have that camera footage analyzed."

"Sounds like a plan." Meanwhile she'd talk to Elmore and get hold of Tyler's birth certificate.

After the bail hearing, she'd pay a visit to Cash's current boss and the place where he'd been living. There might be something in his room to tell her more about Cash.

Good or bad, she had to know before she committed to his defense.

CASH WISHED TO hell he'd had a shower and clean clothes before standing in front of the judge. But he'd had no choice. The sheriff had confiscated his clothing as evidence and given him a county jumpsuit.

Sheriff Jasper shot him a sinister glare as he shoved him in the back of the police car.

Cash had racked his brain to figure out who was bailing him out, and who'd paid for the lawyer, but he didn't dare ask Sheriff Jasper.

He kept his mouth shut on the short drive to the courthouse. Outside, dark clouds hovered as if a storm was gathering on the horizon.

"Judge'll go easier on you if you tell us where the kid is," Sheriff Jasper growled.

Cash choked back a curse. He had to remain calm or the bastard would make things worse for him. "If I knew where he was, I'd tell you."

The sheriff grunted. "If he turns up dead, we're gonna fry you."

Sweat trickled down the side of Cash's face. Outside, the trees swayed in the wind. Even with the breeze, it had to be a hundred degrees.

"Instead of blaming me, why don't you search for Tyler?" Cash said. "If he's with Sondra's killer, he could be in danger. Then that's on you, not me."

Jasper met his gaze in the rearview mirror. Anger slashed the man's jaw. "I got the man who killed his mother right here."

Cash sent him a mutinous look, but remained silent. No use defending himself. Jasper had one mind-set—send him to prison.

They reached the courthouse, and the sheriff parked, then lumbered to the back door to let Cash out. The handcuffs and manacles around his ankles jangled as he walked, but he forced his head up high.

Still, humiliation washed over him as he entered the building. The pretty lawyer lady was waiting. She maintained that professional mask, every damn strand of hair tucked into place.

Did she really believe he was innocent, or was she just doing a job?

It didn't matter. As long as she cleared him, he'd find a way to repay her. Then he'd find Tyler and make sure the kid was safe.

Seconds later, Cash took a seat beside her, his nerves on edge as the bailiff announced the judge's entrance. Silence descended for a moment as the judge, a tall, imposing man with suspicious eyes, reviewed the case file.

Finally, he pounded his gavel and called the session to order. His gaze penetrated Cash like he was pond scum.

Cash's gut churned as the charges were read.

BJ gestured for Cash to stand and he inhaled a breath, willing his legs not to give way.

"Your honor, my name is BJ Alexander. I'm

representing Cash Koker. Due to the fact that he has no priors, and that he's not a flight risk, we're requesting bail be set at ten thousand dollars."

A dark chuckle rumbled from the fiftysomething district attorney. "Your honor, Mr. Koker has been arrested for a brutal murder. Although Miss Alexander claims he's not a flight risk, Mr. Koker has no ties to the community and no family. According to his work history, he's traveled from town to town, even state to state, working odd jobs on different ranches."

Cash tapped his boot on the floor. He hadn't thought his nomadic lifestyle would come back to bite him in the butt.

"For all we know, he may have escape plans in place," the DA continued, "We are requesting bail be denied, and that Mr. Koker be remanded until trial."

The judge checked his notes, then removed his reading glasses and studied Cash.

Cash's breath stalled in his chest. The judge had obviously seen the bloody pictures of Sondra and was going to deny bail.

The door in the back burst open, jarring them. Cash turned to see three men enter, all dressed in Western attire, all big, broad shouldered and tough looking. One wore a sheriff's uniform.

"Your honor, my name is Sheriff Maddox McCullen of Pistol Whip," the tallest of the man said in a deep voice. "May I approach the bench?"

The judge arched his brows in question. "If it pertains to this case, yes."

Sheriff Jasper blustered a protest, but the judge silenced him with a single pound of the gavel. "Approach."

Sheriff McCullen strode toward the judge's galley, the other two men flanking him. As they passed Cash, each of them paused a second to scrutinize him.

Cash tightened his jaw. What the hell was going on?

Did this sheriff have some other trumped-up charges to make sure Cash stayed locked up?

BJ STOOD RAMROD straight in front of the judge beside the McCullens. "Your honor, I've spoken with my client and not only does he claim innocence, he's sincerely worried about the victim's son. The absence of the boy's birth father and his identity suggests that he is a possible suspect."

The judge waved his hand. "We are not trying the case today Miss Alexander. We're here to establish bail."

"Judge," Sheriff McCullen said. "May we speak in chambers?"

The judge rubbed the collar of his robe but nodded. "All right, but you'd better have good reason for this."

"Yes, sir, I do," Maddox said.

BJ and Maddox followed him into his private quarters, leaving Cash looking dumbfounded.

"Now someone explain what's going on?" the judge said as soon as the door was shut.

Maddox cleared his throat. "I realize that you're concerned about Mr. Koker being a flight risk, but I can assure you that he won't flee."

"Just how do you propose to do that?" the judge asked.

"By taking him into my custody," Sheriff McCullen said.

The judge leaned forward. "May I ask why you would do that? What is your involvement with Cash Koker? Has he committed a crime in your jurisdiction?"

"No." Maddox spoke in a low voice. "My brothers and I recently learned that we have twin brothers who were kidnapped at birth. We believe Cash Koker is one of those lost brothers."

The judge raised a brow with interest. "I see. And you plan to blindly take this stranger, who has been accused of murder, into your home? Are you sure that's a wise idea?"

Maddox glanced at BJ, then back to the judge. He was obviously considering her opinion on whether or not Cash was guilty or innocent.

"With all due respect, Judge, my brother Ray is a detective and I'm a lawman," Maddox said. "We'll get to the truth. I promise you that."

"And you'll keep Koker in your custody?"

"Yes, sir," Maddox agreed.

The judge made a clicking sound with his teeth. "All right."

BJ and Maddox followed the judge and bailiff back into the courtroom.

Brett and Ray had taken seats in the courtroom. Cash looked confused and anxious.

"Bail is set at fifty thousand dollars. Mr. Koker, you are released into the custody of Sheriff McCullen." He gave Cash a pointed look. "You are not allowed to leave the county or state. If you have a passport, you will turn it over to the court. If you attempt to flee, you will go back to prison, where you will reside until your trial. Do you understand?"

Cash nodded, his expression wary as he studied Maddox. "Yes, sir, Your Honor."

BJ's stomach knotted as Cash turned accusatory eyes toward her.

He didn't trust her or Maddox.

She certainly couldn't explain here in the courtroom.

The guard released Cash while Brett and Ray went to pay the bail.

"What the hell is your agenda, Sheriff?" Cash growled as the sheriff led him outside then to a police issued SUV. "Did Elmore hire you to get rid of me before the trial?"

# *Chapter Four*

"Just shut up and get in," Sheriff McCullen ordered. "I'll explain later."

The two men who'd been with the sheriff walked down the steps of the courthouse, waved to the sheriff then climbed in a pick-up truck near the sheriff's vehicle.

Cash rubbed his wrists where the handcuffs had been, but he still felt the weight of the metal against his skin.

If they didn't find a way to prove his innocence, he'd go back to jail and stay there the rest of his life. The thought made his lungs squeeze for air.

For a man who liked the open wilderness, country air and the freedom to move around, being confined would kill him.

He tensed as the sheriff veered onto the highway. He had to be prepared in case he drove him into the boonies and tried to get rid of him.

Surely that lawyer lady wouldn't allow him to do something like that. She might not totally believe him, but he'd sensed that she cared about kids and would push the police to hunt for Tyler.

"Where are you taking me?" Cash asked.

Sheriff McCullen glanced at him in the rearview mirror. "To get some of your stuff."

"We're going to the Triple X?"

"Yes. I assumed you'd need clothes."

He did. The stench of blood and now his own body odor was getting to him.

The sheriff veered onto the road leading to the ranch where he'd been working, and Cash noticed the lawyer was following.

"Why did you bail me out?" Cash asked.

The sheriff released a heavy sigh. "We'll discuss that at Horseshoe Creek."

Cash had never been to Horseshoe Creek, but

he'd heard about the McCullen spread. Hell, everyone within five states had heard about it. Apparently the patriarch of the family, Joe McCullen, had run a large cattle and horse operation. He'd died a year ago and left it to his three sons. Maddox was the sheriff. Brett, a big rodeo star. And the youngest, Ray, was a private investigator.

A few months ago, Cash had read an article saying that Joe hadn't died of natural causes as they'd originally thought, but that he'd been murdered.

Joe McCullen and Elmore, Sondra's father, had been rival ranchers, owning two of the largest spreads in this part of Wyoming. Was that why the McCullens were coming to his rescue now? To get back at an old rival?

A sign for the Triple X dangled from wooden posts. The sheriff turned down the drive. Spring had turned to early summer and everything was green. Cows grazed and horses roamed the pastureland. His boss, Wilson Donovan, owned a hundred acres, but that was small compared to the Wagon Wheel and Horseshoe Creek.

With no money for training and breeding, Donovan focused on his cattle.

Tires churned the gravel, bringing Cash closer to the main house and the man who'd taken a chance on him after Elmore had blackballed him in the ranching community.

The sheriff parked and climbed out, then opened Cash's door. Donovan strode down the wooden steps of the rickety porch toward them as BJ pulled her car next to them and got out. Somehow the fact that she'd been following them made Cash feel a bit safer.

A frown pulled Donovan's thick white eyebrows together as he glanced from the sheriff to Cash.

"I'm sorry, Mr. Donovan," Cash began.

Donovan held up a hand. "I'm sorry, too, Cash, but I think you'd better get your stuff and leave."

Cash gritted his teeth, but gave the man a clipped nod. Dammit. Donovan had taken a chance on him, and he'd failed him.

How the hell was he going to pay Sheriff McCullen back for his bail if he had no job or income?

BJ WANTED TO question Donovan without Cash present.

"I'll accompany Cash to his quarters so he can retrieve his clothes," Maddox offered.

Cash glared at him. "You think I'm going to run?"

Maddox crossed his arms. "Are you?"

Anger flashed across Cash's face. "No."

BJ traded a knowing look with Maddox. "Mr. Donovan and I will join you at his cabin."

"Bunkhouses are about a mile from the main house," Donovan said. "Sheriff Jasper already come out and searched Cash's room."

Cash heaved a weary breath. "Of course he did."

BJ made a mental note to ask Jasper about the search.

Maddox motioned for Cash to get back in the

car, and he did so. But he looked irritated and worried. Did he have something to hide?

Donovan tipped his hat. "You think Cash killed the woman?"

BJ shrugged slightly "He claims he didn't, that he and Sondra were only friends." She paused to see if he reacted, but he didn't, so she continued. "The woman's three-year-old son is missing. Cash is afraid someone kidnapped him. What do you think about Cash?"

"I know what Elmore said, but I liked Cash. He was a hard worker and seemed honest." Donovan worked his mouth from side to side. "Elmore's cutthroat to us smaller ranchers. He was also protective of his daughter. Hell, I figured he'd kill anyone who touched her."

Interesting. His opinion backed up Cash's story. "Did Sondra visit Cash here at the ranch?"

"She dropped her kid off a few times," Donovan said. "But I don't know what happened between them. What the hands do on their time off is their business, long as they don't bring trouble here." He hesitated. "You might ask Hanks, Cash's bunkmate."

"I will. And if you don't mind, I'd like to talk to some of your other ranch hands."

Donovan scratched his chin. "Feel free. I'd like to see Cash catch a break. But unfortunately, I can't keep him on here. The negative publicity is bad for business, and business is bad enough as it is."

"Thanks." Donovan sounded like a fair man. "Is there anything else you can tell me about Cash?"

"I never seen anyone ride like him. He has a knack for herding, too." He removed his hat and ran a hand through his thinning hair. "Cash is ambitious. I think it's always bugged him that he's not in charge. Was saving up to buy his own land someday."

His earlier comment replayed in her head. "You said you figured Elmore would kill any man who touched his daughter. Do you think Elmore was dangerous?"

"I can't say." Donovan shrugged. "Elmore was

ruthless in business, and he ran some guys off. Two of my hands before Cash used to work there. Said he fired them for flirting with his daughter."

"What about Elmore's grandson, Tyler?"

"Cash adored that kid and took him riding. But Elmore didn't talk about Tyler." The rancher adjusted his hat on his head. "Thought that was odd. Most grandparents gush over their young 'uns."

"Did you see Elmore often?"

Donovan shook his head. "Just at the Cattleman's Club. He kept to business, though."

"Elmore thought Cash was Tyler's father, but he claims he's not. Do you have any idea who the boy's father is?"

Confusion clouded the man's eyes. "No. Like I said, Elmore stuck to work."

Did Elmore have any real friends?

And how about enemies?

If Elmore gave his rivals a difficult time, one of them could have cozied up to Sondra to get back at Elmore. If so, and Sondra found out she'd been used, she wouldn't have wanted her father to know.

That would explain the reason she'd lied about Tyler's father being Cash.

CASH CLIMBED FROM the police car at the bunkhouse, his instincts alert. He should be grateful this sheriff had stopped to let him pack his things.

He wished he could get his truck. But Jasper had had it impounded and searched for forensic evidence.

Maddox grunted as he walked toward the bunkhouse. Dammit, he still had no idea what the man's agenda was. Strangers in these parts didn't just up and pay fifty thousand dollars to help murder suspects, much less take one into their home. Did Maddox McCullen want to help him or find the evidence to lock him away for life?

Each bunkhouse held two rooms, with a common bathroom. His bunkmate, Will Hanks, was out working the herd, so the place was empty.

The sheriff entered first. A muscle ticked in his jaw as he glanced at Cash. "Looks like Sheriff Jasper did more than search the room."

Rage mushroomed inside Cash. The room looked as if it had been tossed. The dresser drawers holding his clothes were open, his clothing spilling out. The few books he had were dumped on the floor, some of the pages bent and torn as if someone had searched between them. His ranching magazines were scattered everywhere, as well.

The sheriff strode through the room, skimming the surfaces. Cash had no idea what he expected to find. He had no personal photographs. No mementos of his past.

Nothing in his past was worth holding on to.

If there had been anything of interest, Jasper had already removed it.

The closet was just as big a mess. The shoebox on the top shelf that held his personal papers had been pilfered through. His checkbook and the envelope with cash in it were there, but his business plan was gone.

Why would the sheriff take that? It had nothing to do with Sondra.

Thankfully, his guitar was standing against the wall in the closet. His heart hammered, though, as he knelt to check beneath his bed for his guns. Both missing.

"What is it?" the sheriff asked.

Cash swallowed hard. "My guns are missing."

The man narrowed his eyes. "What kind and how many?"

"A rifle and a pistol."

"I'll ask Sheriff Jasper if he confiscated them. Have they been used lately?"

Cash rubbed his forehead, grateful he had backups. "I fired the rifle a few days ago at a snake when we were herding."

A quick nod of his head was the man's only reaction. "Pack some clothes while I make the call."

Phone in hand, the sheriff stepped outside.

Cash yanked his duffel bag from the closet, then retrieved the extra pistol he kept in the storage compartment beneath the floor. Thankfully Jasper hadn't noticed the rug covering the spot.

Granted he'd get in trouble for having it since he was out on bail, but he might need it for protection.

He couldn't rely on anyone else.

He piled his clothes on top. Jeans, work shirts, a couple dressy Western shirts, an extra pair of work boots. Even though it was summer and he didn't need it, he grabbed his long duster. Basically, it was everything he owned.

Because he wouldn't be coming back.

His toiletries went into a toiletry bag and he was ready to go.

He took one last look at the bunkhouse room and wondered what the sheriff had thought he would find under the mattress.

Jasper had probably been disappointed that Cash didn't have incriminating pictures of himself and Sondra or a damn journal describing how he planned to kill her. Instead, he'd found Cash's business plan, not a blueprint for murder or kidnapping.

Still, he had that damn video of Cash entering

the motel where Sondra had died. And his knife with his bloody fingerprints on it.

Frustration blended with fear.

That might be enough to put him away for life.

BJ STUDIED DONOVAN. "We think the little boy's birth father might have something to do with his mother's murder. Finding him could be key to proving Cash's innocence."

Donovan leaned heavily on his left leg as if his other was hurting. "I told you, I got no idea."

"Did something happen between you and Elmore?" BJ asked. "Did he try to sabotage your business?"

Donovan shook his head. "I'm small potatoes. He offered to buy me out once, but I turned him down." He gazed across the ranch. "I love this place. It's home."

"Did he pressure you?"

"No. No need to. I certainly wasn't any competition for him." He gestured toward his truck. "The hands should be at the dining hall for lunch. I'll drive you over so you can talk to 'em."

BJ studied his face. He seemed genuine, as if he held no grudge against Elmore.

BJ climbed in the passenger side. The truck was old but clean, the motor humming as he drove the half mile to the dining hall. The rustic building boasted a big cowbell in front. The ranch hands were lining up on the porch and trickling inside.

The scent of barbecue drifted to her as soon as she climbed from the truck.

As they entered, she counted ten men in line, and a cook and two helpers were setting out trays of buns, barbecue, coleslaw and baked beans. Another station held water, milk, coffee, tea and lemonade.

"There's Will Hanks," Donovan said. "He shares the bunkhouse with Cash."

BJ scrutinized the tall, lean cowboy. Probably in his twenties. Good-looking with an air of confidence. A flirtatious gleam lit his eyes as his gaze met hers.

"This is BJ Alexander. She's Cash's attorney," Donovan said.

Hanks's smile wilted slightly. "They think he killed Sondra Elmore, right?"

"Those are the charges," BJ said. "Why? Do you have information regarding the case?"

He shifted from foot to foot, then looked away. "I don't think Cash is a killer. But he liked that woman and her kid."

"Was Cash violent?" BJ asked.

He grabbed a tray. "I don't know. He had a rough childhood," Hanks said. "One of his foster fathers beat him a lot. That'd make a man angry."

BJ's heart squeezed. She'd heard horror stories of foster care. "Did he talk about Elmore?"

The man added extra barbecue sauce to his bun. "He said Elmore reminded him of that foster father."

Hmm, that comment could work against Cash in court.

"Do you know who fathered Sondra Elmore's child?"

He shook his head. "No, ma'am."

They talked for another minute as he filled his tray, but he had nothing bad to say about Cash.

Just as she was about to join Donovan again, another cowboy approached her.

This man was shorter and introduced himself as Hyatt Spillman. "You asking about Cash Koker?"

She nodded. "What can you tell me?" she said as they stepped onto the porch.

He shuffled a toothpick in the corner of his mouth. "I heard a phone conversation between Koker and that woman Sondra the morning of the day she died. They were arguing."

BJ's pulse jumped. "What did they argue about?"

He made a clicking sound with his teeth. "I couldn't hear what she said, but he told her he loved her and promised to take care of her and her kid."

BJ crossed her arms in front of her chest. "Go on."

"She must have turned him down, 'cause he got mad. Told her he'd never let her go."

Anger seeped through BJ.

Cash had lied about being in love with Sondra. And they'd argued the day she died.

What if he'd flown into a rage because she wanted him out of her and Tyler's life, and he killed her in a fit of passion?

Spillman's story brought up all sorts of doubts. She couldn't automatically rely on the man, because it was clear someone could be trying to frame Cash.

But if not…

She was going to have to be extra thorough on this one to get to the truth. And not let Cash's attachment to Tyler cause her to free another guilty murderer.

# *Chapter Five*

BJ texted Maddox and asked him to meet her at the dining hall.

"Thank you for your cooperation, Mr. Spillman." She handed him a business card. "If you think of anything that can shed light on Sondra Elmore's death, please call me."

He tapped the card against his hand. "You be careful, Miss Alexander. I'd hate to see the same thing that happened to Sondra happen to you."

The hair on the back of her neck prickled. Was that a threat? Or a warning about Cash?

Maddox pulled up with a grim-looking Cash in the back.

"Did you find anything?" she asked when he rolled down his window.

"Jasper already thoroughly searched the place. If there was anything there, he confiscated it."

"If he says he found something, he planted it," Cash said in a voice laced with anger. "I told you I didn't kill Sondra."

"I'll call Jasper." BJ entered the sheriff's number into her phone, her own temper close to the surface. "This is BJ Alexander. I need to know everything you found when you searched Cash Koker's bunkhouse."

"I don't have to tell you anything," Sheriff Jasper barked.

"Yes, you do. Before the trial, you're required to disclose all evidence to the defense attorney. That's me. So why don't you make both our lives easier and do it now?"

Jasper cursed. "All right, lady. We found pictures of Mr. Koker and Sondra. Looks like they were all lovey-dovey."

She twisted to look at Cash, her pulse clamoring. "Explain."

"They were wrapped up in each other's arms."

Cash had denied being romantically involved with Sondra. "Text me a copy. I need to see them myself. What else?"

"Ask him about my business plan," Cash said from the backseat. "And my guns."

BJ gripped the phone tighter. "Did you find a business plan?"

"Sure did," Jasper said. "Koker needed finances to make that happen. My guess is he hated Elmore for firing him and decided to use that kid for blackmail money to buy his own spread."

BJ bit her bottom lip. She and Cash had discussed a blackmail accusation back at the jail, but he hadn't disclosed his plans to start his own business. Unfortunately, jurors might see that as a motive.

"What about Koker's guns?"

"Took them for analysis," Jasper said. "Besides, a dangerous man like him doesn't need firearms in his possession."

BJ gritted her teeth. "What about other suspects?"

"Listen, Ms. Alexander, we have motive and physical evidence. We got the right man."

"We'll see." BJ ended the call, irritated.

Jasper did have a case. No doubt he'd twist the fact that Cash claimed he had amnesia to suggest he was lying. The ranch hand's testimony about that phone call between Cash and Sondra would also be incriminating.

Damn. With motive and physical evidence, Jasper might get a conviction.

CASH WAS SHOCKED that Sheriff McCullen went by the impound lot and allowed him to retrieve his pickup truck.

"Just follow me to the ranch," Sheriff McCullen said. "You can stay at Horseshoe Creek until the case is over. Miss Alexander is already staying in a cabin on the ranch."

Suspicion once again flared inside Cash. Nobody helped a stranger for nothing. He'd just have to bide his time until he figured out what the sheriff wanted.

Questions nagged at him as he followed the

police SUV. Farm and ranch lands spread for miles and miles, the open space beckoning.

He could not give up his freedom. He'd rather die than be locked away for the rest of his life.

All the more reason he find out who'd framed him and killed Sondra. Poor little Tyler—he must be scared out of his mind.

Sweat beaded on Cash's neck. The cards were stacked against him, though. How hard would BJ Alexander fight to get him acquitted?

And what the hell did any of this have to do with the McCullens?

A sign for Horseshoe Creek Ranch mocked him as the sheriff veered down a long drive. The lawyer lady followed in her fancy car.

Cattle grazed in a pasture to the north and barns and horses were scattered throughout the beautiful farmland. An article a few months ago had featured Brett McCullen, former rodeo star, and his awards. He'd also expanded the ranch to include horse training and breeding. His popularity and skills definitely drew customers, and his contacts across the states aided in him securing the best horses.

Elmore had an impressive spread, but he'd talked about Joe McCullen with both admiration and resentment. McCullen had built a legacy for his sons—a fact Elmore envied. Sondra hadn't cared about the ranch business, and Elmore had never had a son.

The sheriff drove toward the main ranch house, an impressive farmhouse with wraparound porches that sat on a hill overlooking the massive acreage. He bypassed the house, though, and veered onto a lane that weaved through the property. A half mile from the house, several smaller cabins had been built for employees or guests. Sheriff McCullen pulled in front of one and parked. Cash swung his truck in beside him, then the lawyer parked on the other side.

"This is where you'll be staying, Cash," Sheriff McCullen said.

Cash straightened. "I don't understand why you're doing this, Sheriff."

The sheriff and lawyer exchanged a look. "Get cleaned up, then we'll meet in the main house to discuss the situation."

"You mean you trust me to stay here alone, or do you have a guard dog on me?" Cash asked.

The sheriff folded his arms. "Are you going to jump bail?"

Cash bit the inside of his cheek. His flight reflex was strong. How many times had he moved when things became sticky or uncomfortable where he was?

Too many to count.

But if he ran from this, the law would hunt him down. And he needed help finding Tyler.

"No." He swallowed hard. "I intend to clear my name." It was the only way he'd be free. "Tyler needs me, too. That kid has to be scared."

The sheriff's gaze met his, some kind of emotion flickering in his eyes that Cash couldn't read. "All right then." He gestured toward Miss Alexander. "Let's meet in half an hour at the house."

She agreed and Cash nodded. Then maybe he'd finally learn what the McCullens wanted with him.

BJ BATTLED HER uneasiness at sleeping in a cabin in close proximity to Cash. He thought she was afraid of him because she believed him guilty of murder.

But that wasn't the problem. Cash Koker was too sexy.

Sexy men were dangerous.

She stepped onto the porch of the cabin where she'd been staying, phoned her father and left a message updating him. A breeze ruffled the leaves on the trees, bringing her the scent of wildflowers and freshly cut grass. Rays of sunshine slanted across the ranch, the sky so beautiful that it nearly robbed her breath.

And reminded her of Aaron's rainbows.

She allowed herself a second to imagine him running across the field, then forced the image at bay. Work always helped take her mind off her grief.

Work was all she had.

The McCullens had lived here for decades, but they'd suffered their share of loss, both with the murder of their mother, and then the loss of their father to questionable circumstances. Yet they'd found a way to stay together as a family.

She wasn't sure she could say the same about her own father. All her life, she'd craved his love. She'd tried to please him and make him proud, but nothing she did brought them any closer.

Sometimes, she thought he blamed her for her mother's death, that he wished she'd never been born.

And although he hadn't said much about her mistake with the Davis case, she had disappointed him.

She slipped into the cabin and surveyed the interior, admiring the space for its hominess. Painted wood-paneled walls. A kitchen and an adjoining living area with a stone fireplace. Bathroom and bedroom complete with a queen four-poster bed draped in a country blue quilt.

Feeling overdressed, she considered a change of clothes.

But she hadn't brought anything casual enough to wear on a ranch. No jeans or flannel shirts or cowboy boots.

She went to freshen up and stared at herself in the mirror. It didn't matter if she had ranch clothes. Or if she wore her hair pulled back in a tight bun.

Or if Cash Koker thought she was a stuffy bitch.

She was here to do a job and nothing more.

Her phone dinged, alerting her that she had a text, and she rushed to see it. Anger hit her as a photo of Cash and Sondra hugging appeared on her screen.

Sheriff Jasper was right. The two of them looked close in the picture, a lot closer than Cash had led her to believe.

But pictures could be deceiving.

Still, she was more confused than ever by the man in the cabin next to her.

CASH THREW THE prison clothes into the trash and strode naked to the shower, anxious to rid himself of the scent of Sondra's blood.

How in the hell could he have gotten her blood on his clothes and hands and not remember it?

He closed his eyes as he scrubbed his body and hair, trying to force the memory to return, but his mind was a big black hole.

So was his heart. Sondra had been his friend, Innocent. Young. Vibrant. In love with life. She had a bright future ahead of her.

And she'd loved Tyler so much.

He would miss her smile and chatter.

An image of little Tyler laughing as he pushed him in the tire swing Cash had made for him taunted him.

Emotions churned through him. He'd kill anyone who hurt that kid.

Heart hammering, he dried off and dressed in clean jeans and a denim shirt.

Anxious to hear the sheriff's explanation, he snatched his wallet and stepped outside.

The fresh air and scents of summer hit him,

then the door to the cabin where the lawyer was staying opened. Sun slanted off her pale skin, giving her a radiant glow.

She was still wearing that tight-assed suit, but even though it was modest, it didn't disguise her curves. Nice sized breasts, a thin waist, hips a man could hold on to.

Dammit, his body twitched with desire.

Not a good thing.

She held the key to his freedom. He couldn't screw it up by screwing her.

Squaring his shoulders, he strode toward her.

Her eyes flickered with wariness as she met him on the path between their cabins. "Ready?"

He nodded, willing his libido under control. If he made a wrong move toward her, she might drop his case.

At the moment, he needed her brains more than he needed her body.

But could he trust that she wasn't working for the enemy?

"We can take my car," she offered.

"I'd just as soon walk." He needed the fresh air.

"Sure."

She fell into step beside him although she was wearing heels, which slowed her pace, so he slowed his own so she could keep up.

He'd like to see her in a pair of tight jeans, but he refrained from comment.

An awkward silence stretched between them as they followed the drive to the main house. By the time they reached it, she was wobbly on those heels. She stumbled, and he caught her arm. She felt small and delicate next to him, and she smelled so damn feminine, like jasmine, that it stirred images of making love to her in a bed of wildflowers.

Her gaze met his, a warning in those eyes, and he dropped his hand.

Idiot. A woman like her wouldn't be caught dead in his bed, much less naked in a field of wildflowers with him.

The thought made his anger rise again. "Sorry, Miss Alexander. I was just trying to help."

She paused, lips forming a thin line as she stared him down. "It's BJ."

"BJ?"

"Yes, that's my name," she said, with a bite to her voice. "If we're going to work together, you can't keep calling me Miss Alexander like it's a dirty word."

A smile tugged at his lips. "All right, BJ." He liked the way it rolled off his tongue. "So why the initials? What does BJ stand for?"

"None of your business." She tossed him a withering smile, dispelling any semblance that she planned to get friendly, then walked ahead and climbed the porch steps. He followed like a damn dog in heat.

A chubby lady with a warm smile greeted them, and introduced herself as Mama Mary, the housekeeper and cook. She studied Cash for a moment as if she was dissecting him, then her eyes twinkled. "Nice to meet you, Mr. Cash. Y'all come on in and make yourselves at home." She shook the lawyer's hand, then Cash's, her gaze lingering on him, welcoming. Friendly.

An odd reaction, since she must be aware he'd been arrested for murder.

Remembering his manners, he tipped his Stetson. He'd felt naked without it in jail.

She directed them toward a closed door. "I'll get some coffee for everyone and sandwiches, and I just made a cobbler."

Cash didn't think his arrest warranted cobbler, but he was starving so he kept his mouth shut.

Voices from inside the room echoed through the wall. "You think he's innocent?"

"I don't know, but we'll find out." That voice belonged to the sheriff.

"I don't think we should tell him who we are, not yet," a third man said.

Anger gripped Cash, and he stormed through the door. He didn't intend to be in the dark another minute.

# *Chapter Six*

Tension vibrated through the room as Cash faced the McCullen men. If these men were his enemies, he had a right to know.

Sheriff McCullen and his brothers exchanged odd looks, an awkwardness heating the air.

"Why did you bail me out and bring me here?" Cash demanded. "What do you want from me?"

The sheriff cleared his throat. "I'm Maddox, and this is Brett and Ray."

"I know who you are," Cash said between gritted teeth.

"You do?" Ray said, brows raised.

"Of course." Cash frowned. "Everyone in this

part of Wyoming knows the McCullens own Horseshoe Creek."

The men traded looks again.

"What else do you know about us?" Maddox asked.

Another inquisition? "The story about your father's murder was all over the news." He folded his arms. "Now, answer my question. Why did you bring me here? Are you in cahoots with Elmore?"

Surprise flared on the men's faces. "Why would you ask that?" Ray said.

"Because you don't know me and I don't know you," Cash said. "Yet you posted my bail. Maybe you're working with him or whoever's framing me."

"Good God," Ray said. "You can't be serious."

"I work for the people of Pistol Whip and this county," Maddox said stiffly. "My job is to uphold the law. I can't be bought."

The lawyer touched Cash's arm. "Cash, trust me, they aren't here to hurt you. They want the truth, the same as you and I do."

He whirled around, his pent-up rage exploding. "Look, lady, in my experience, no one comes out of the woodwork to help someone, especially not someone like me. Not without his or her own agenda."

A heartbeat of silence passed. A knock sounded, and Mama Mary appeared with a tray. Her bubbly smile seemed at odds with the tension in the air.

"Hey, boys. I have food and coffee."

Cash crossed the room to the window and stared out at the horses galloping on a hill in the distance, while Mama Mary set the food on a bar by the wall.

"Thanks, Mama Mary." Brett gave her a hug. "You're the best."

Heat flushed Cash's neck. Everything he'd read about the McCullens indicated they were honest folks. So why all the secrecy?

Mama Mary closed the door of the study as she left, and Maddox gestured toward the sitting area. "Sit down, Cash, and we'll explain."

He jammed his hands into the pockets of his jeans as the McCullens seated themselves.

Still on edge, Cash hesitated, but the lawyer gestured to two wing chairs. She sank into one, and he finally relented and took the other.

"Coffee?" Maddox asked.

"Not until you give me some answers."

Maddox's gaze skated over him. "All right. We paid your bail and brought you here because we wanted to get to know you, to find out if you killed Sondra Elmore."

Cash swallowed hard. "I didn't. But why do you care? I thought you and Elmore were rivals."

Maddox shrugged. "He and my dad were, but we've made peace between the families."

"So you're trying to help him by wringing a confession out of me?"

"No." Maddox glanced at his brothers, then leaned back in his chair. "Last year, when we learned our father was murdered, we also discovered that our mother's death wasn't an accident."

He had no idea where they were going with this. "I had nothing to do with that."

"Man, you are paranoid," Ray said.

"We aren't implying that you did," Brett added.

Cash studied them, confused.

"Just listen," Sheriff McCullen said gruffly. "Our mother was murdered because of twin boys she gave birth to."

"Her doctor told my parents that the babies died at birth, and that he cremated them," Brett said. "But they didn't die."

"They were kidnapped," Ray said. "Once we realized they'd survived, we started searching for them. They were left at a church. One of the babies was adopted, although I haven't tracked his adopted parents down yet." He hesitated. "The other baby was sickly and ended up in foster care."

Cash's head spun as he tried to keep up. *He'd grown up in foster care…*

The sheriff folded his hands and leaned forward, pinning Cash with his dark gaze. "Cash, we believe you may be one of the twins."

WHATEVER DOUBTS BJ had that Cash knew about his relationship to the McCullens faded. The shock on his face was so real that compassion flooded her.

In the past three days he'd been accused of murdering his friend and kidnapping her son, had been locked in a cell, crucified by Sheriff Jasper and bailed out by virtual strangers.

It was no surprise that, after a lifetime of injustices, he was suspicious of their motives. He'd been raised in foster care, shuffled from one place to another, then fired by Elmore for fathering Tyler, when he wasn't the father.

"I don't believe it." Cash's voice cracked. "Is this some kind of sick joke?"

"We wouldn't kid about something this serious," Ray said curtly.

"Of course, we want to run DNA to confirm," Maddox said matter-of-factly.

"We can also use that test to prove you didn't father Tyler," BJ said.

Cash scrutinized each brother, one at a time, as if searching for the lies in their eyes. Then he turned to BJ, as if in the midst of the madness, she was the one he trusted.

An awkward silence filled the room while Cash absorbed what they'd told him.

"I don't know what to say," he finally muttered.

Ray cleared his throat. "What did the social workers or your foster parents tell you about your past?"

Cash shrugged. "Nothing. Just that someone abandoned me on the steps of a church."

"Did they mention that you had a twin?" Brett asked.

Cash shook his head, his face strained with shock. "No, nothing about any siblings or family."

"Like Maddox said, we'll check DNA," Ray said, "but if you are a McCullen, you have a twin."

Cash dropped his head into his hands and rubbed his forehead. When he looked up at them, pain darkened his eyes. "That's the reason you posted my bail? Because you think I'm a Mc…Cullen?"

Maddox exhaled. "Yes. And if DNA proves you are, we'll do everything we can to help you."

Maddox hesitated, his voice hard when he continued. “Although, brother or not, if you killed that woman, we won’t cover for you.”

Cash stood, his pulse pounding. “I didn’t kill her. And I sure as hell didn’t take Tyler. I don’t care what happens to me, but I want you to find that little boy.”

Maddox and his brothers traded another conspiratorial look. Then Maddox went to his desk. “Then let’s take that DNA sample and send it to the lab. It sounds like we’ve got our work cut out for us.”

CASH’S HEAD WAS reeling as Maddox swabbed the inside of his cheek. The last thing in the world he’d expected to hear was that these men thought he was related to them.

Or that he had a twin.

Shock mixed with bitterness. All these years he’d been alone, had no family, no one who gave a damn about him. But he might have three brothers and another one out there somewhere who, like him, had no idea who he was.

Had his twin found a home with a family? Maybe his life had been better than Cash's.

Or maybe he wasn't a McCullen at all and this conversation was a big mistake.

He wouldn't get his hopes up.

Still, he needed help to clear himself.

Maddox bagged the swab. "We'll have that run ASAP. Now, we need to address the charges and the evidence against you."

BJ lifted a finger. "I phoned Sheriff Jasper. He forwarded a photo he found of you and Sondra together, Cash." She removed her phone from her pocket and showed him the text. "It looks like the two of you are cozy."

Cash's eyes widened. "I don't know who took that, but it's not what it seems."

"You and Sondra are in each other's arms," BJ said.

Cash studied the photograph again. "She was upset that day," he said. "Her father sent her away for a while to hide the pregnancy, but she came back and announced that she was keeping the baby. Elmore pressured her to give Tyler up for adoption, said he'd make arrangements to keep it quiet so she could resume her place in society by his side."

He made a sound of disgust. "She didn't give a flip about society. She came crying to me because she knew I grew up in foster care, and that I'd be sympathetic."

"And you were?" Brett said quietly.

"Damn right I was." Anger gripped him. "I always figured my mother gave me up because she was a teenager or didn't have money to raise me. Lester Elmore had plenty of money and a big house and could have hired a damned nanny for Sondra if he wanted. There was no reason to give that little boy to strangers when Sondra wanted to keep him."

"You didn't sleep with her?" Maddox asked bluntly.

"No," Cash said just as bluntly. "Never."

Maddox set a laptop on the table in the middle of the seating area. "I asked for copies of the evidence Sheriff Jasper had against you, and received a copy of the video camera footage. It showed you entering the motel where Sondra's body was found."

Cash's stomach roiled. How could he possibly disprove all this physical evidence?

Maddox pointed to the screen. "Look at it, Cash. Tell me what you see and what you remember."

Cash scooted his chair closer to the computer, and the others gathered around to look. A sick feeling churned in his gut.

Shadows hovered around the outside of the room, the moon barely a sliver in the sky, making it appear eerily dark.

The camera time indicated it was after midnight, twelve fifteen to be exact.

But there he was. Standing at the edge of the bushes by the motel room, a Stetson pulled low on his head, his face cast downward as if avoiding the camera.

The sheriff had been sure it was him, but how could he be when his face was in the shadows?

He mentally retraced what he remembered

from that night. He was wearing jeans and the shirt he'd been arrested it. In the photo, it looked like the same shirt, but something was different.

"Is there any way you can enhance the picture?" Cash asked.

Maddox shrugged as if to say no, but Ray tapped some keys and enlarged the shot.

"The time on the photo says twelve fifteen." Cash drummed his fingers on his thigh. "Sondra called me about ten. She was upset and asked me to meet her. I got to the tavern around ten thirty."

"What happened next?" BJ asked.

"I ordered a whiskey and drank it."

"Did you talk to anyone?" Maddox asked.

Cash strained to remember. "The bartender. I think his name was Henry."

"Anyone else?" Ray asked.

He struggled to recall, but the details were fuzzy. "Not anyone in particular. The bar was packed. Sondra rushed in and was frantic. We ordered drinks, then she wanted to go outside to talk." He rubbed his forehead, his fingers tracing the jagged scar, a reminder of where he'd come from. He'd let his hair grow a little shaggy, but nothing could hide it. "I remember heading into the alley and then…everything goes black."

Ray clicked a few more keys, and zoomed in on his head in the camera shot.

Cash's heart hammered. It was difficult to see his face with the Stetson on, a hat exactly like his, but…his scar…where was it?

"Do you see what I see?" he asked.

Maddox grunted. "What?"

"That's not me," Cash said.

"It sure as hell looks like you," Brett said.

Cash removed his hat, laid it on his lap and pushed the hair away from his forehead. His scar ran from the top of his skull in a jagged, curvy line and wrapped around behind his right ear.

"By God, you're right," Ray said. "The man in this video footage has no scar."

"He looks shorter, too," Maddox pointed out.

For the first time since his arrest, hope shot through Cash. The picture proved he wasn't at the door of the motel during the time frame of Sondra's death.

Which meant that someone had framed him for murder.

# *Chapter Seven*

Questions bombarded Cash.

The idea that he had a twin struck him like a fist in the gut. Did his twin know about him? Could he have been at the motel?

Or was another man pretending to be him?

Who hated him enough to set him up for murder?

And how had he ended up in that room next to Sondra's dead body? Had someone knocked him out or drugged him and put him there?

"I'm going to find our other brother," Ray said. "And I'll figure out who this is in the picture."

"It's time we talk to Elmore," Maddox said. "If

he received a ransom demand, maybe it'll lead us to Sondra's killer."

Emotions ping-ponged inside Cash. He didn't know how to respond. All his life he'd been on his own.

Did these men really believe him? Were they actually going to help him?

Brett walked over to the bar where Mama Mary had left the food and coffee. "I say we chow down before you go. Mama Mary went to a lot of trouble for us."

"You know she loves it," Ray said with a twinkle in his eye.

"She's been with us since we were kids," Maddox said to Cash. "She took care of us when Mama died."

Envy stirred inside Cash. These men looked slightly different but had similar features—strong jaws and high cheekbones, tanned skin, dark hair—just like his own. Yet they'd grown up together, had wrestled as boys, had shared memories with their parents. Had bonded.

If he was their brother, he'd lost years of being with them.

How would his life have been different if he'd grown up on Horseshoe Creek? If he'd had family? Someone who gave a damn.

*If* he was their brother. That was still the operative word. He still couldn't believe it.

Maddox motioned to BJ and him. "Come on and grab a plate."

BJ stepped to the bar, poured a cup of coffee and choose a sandwich from the tray. Cash's stomach growled. He'd hardly eaten since the arrest. The grub Sheriff Jasper had shoved in the cell could hardly be called food.

Cash poured himself a cup of coffee, then chose a hearty roast beef sandwich.

"Take all you want," Brett said. "Mama Mary will be offended if we don't clean this tray."

The men's affection for the older woman was obvious.

He grabbed a second sandwich, then scooped potato salad into a bowl and carried his plate and coffee over to the long table at the far end of the study. He sat awkwardly, waiting on the McCullens to fill their plates.

The scene was almost surreal. He'd come here suspicious of their motives, but as far as he could tell, they'd been honest. And now they were sharing a meal like…a real family.

Cash's throat closed. He'd never had a real family.

What if he wasn't one of them?

Or what if he was and he let them down? Would they claim him as blood kin if he ended up in prison for the rest of his life?

BJ SIPPED HER COFFEE, well aware of Cash's discomfort. She felt slightly awkward herself.

This family was nothing like her own. Her father was stiff and formal. She'd been raised by nannies and housekeepers who were stuffy and rigid, not loving and friendly like Mama Mary, who felt more like a family member than an employee.

Maddox folded his hands prayer-style. "Let's say grace."

Following the men's lead, she folded her hands and bowed her head. Cash took a second longer, his posture stiff, as if saying a blessing was a foreign concept to him.

Maddox blessed the food, then the men dug in with gusto. Cash finally relaxed, and judging from how quickly he scarfed down his food, he hadn't eaten in days.

He'd been locked up by Jasper, who had made no bones about his dislike for Cash.

"Did Sondra say anything to you about Tyler when she met you at the bar?"

Cash wiped his mouth with a napkin. "No, we barely talked. It was loud in the bar so she pulled me outside."

"Then you blacked out?" Ray asked.

Cash exhaled, then rubbed the back of his head. "Yeah. I thought someone might have hit me in the back of the head, but there's no bump."

"You could have been drugged," BJ pointed out. Maddox cursed. "Jasper should have had your blood tested, but he didn't."

"What about Sondra's friends? Did she have a

close girlfriend she might have left Tyler with?" BJ asked.

"She had more guy friends than girlfriends," Cash said. "But she kept in touch with some girl named Diane."

"You know her last name?" Maddox asked.

Cash shook his head.

"I saw a post with her on Facebook," BJ said.

"Jasper probably talked to her, but we'll follow up." Maddox polished off his food.

"He won't like your interference," BJ said.

"I don't care," Maddox said. "I don't trust him. I know a judge who will agree with me, too." He stood, shifting back and forth, obviously antsy. "Besides, the murder occurred in Sheriff Jasper's jurisdiction but technically the Elmore's live in mine so I have to investigate the kidnapping."

So he could justify his involvement.

"I'm going to question Elmore myself." BJ turned to Cash. "I think you should go, too. I want to see Elmore's reaction."

"I need to check on Rose and the baby first." Maddox pushed back from the table.

"We have some new quarter horses coming in. I have to be here," Brett said.

Ray set down his fork. "I'll work on identifying this guy in the camera. We find him, he can fill us in on what really happened that night."

BJ's mind raced. What if that man was his twin and he'd set him up? Although why would he do that?

Maddox folded his napkin and placed it on his plate. "If you get an address, call me and I'll pick him up."

"Thank you for lunch," BJ said.

"Yes, thanks," Cash said. "And please thank Mama Mary for me. That's the best meal I've had in a long time."

"Hell, if you think that was good, you should taste Mama Mary's chicken 'n dumplings," Brett said.

Maddox rubbed his belly and Ray muttered an *Amen*.

BJ's heart melted at the uncertainty in Cash's eyes. For a man who'd never had a family, becoming part of this close-knit group could be something special.

But they needed the DNA test first. And they had to prove Cash's innocence and find Tyler.

She didn't know the child, but she was worried sick about him.

With Jasper's stubbornness about Cash's guilt, they'd already lost precious time tracking down the child.

She only hoped Tyler didn't end up like Sondra.

CASH TAMPED DOWN any smidgen of hope that he belonged to this family. Things like that didn't happen to people like him.

Loser. That's what his foster father used to call him.

Not that he cared about that bastard's opinion. But he had believed it as a kid.

Then he'd met this social worker named Darma who'd told him he could wallow in pity or be the man he wanted to be.

He'd taken her advice and learned ranching

skills. He'd even enrolled in business classes to help him if he ever could afford his own spread.

Mama Mary bustled in to get the dirty dishes, and he thanked her for the food.

She looked him up and down for a moment, as if trying to decide if he was who they thought he was, then her plump cheeks turned rosy with her smile. "You're certainly welcome, Mr. Cash. It's nice to meet you."

Nice to meet him? He was under arrest.

He tipped his hat. "You, too, ma'am. You're a fine cook."

Her smile widened, the dimples in her cheeks deepening. "I don't have to wait on DNA. You've got more of your mama in you than the other boys." She pressed a hand to his cheek. "She was a good woman and loved the other three boys. But when that doctor told her she lost those twins, it tore her up something bad."

Cash had always wondered if his mother regretted giving him up. If she'd thought about him over the years, or missed him, or even remembered him on his birthday.

If he'd been kidnapped at birth and was part of this family, it meant his mother had loved him. That she'd grieved when he'd been taken.

Sadness welled in his chest.

BJ stepped back. "We'll meet Maddox at Elmore's," she said. "It'll take time to get those warrants. I'm anxious to see if Elmore has received any word about Tyler."

She led the way through the house and outside.

Maddox had taken him off guard with that blessing. Cash didn't pray often.

But he said a silent prayer that Tyler was still alive, and that he'd been found as they headed to her car.

BJ CALLED SHERIFF Jasper as she slid into the driver's seat. The phone rang four times, then his voice mail picked up. "Sheriff Jasper, it's BJ Alexander. Call me with an update on the Amber Alert."

She ended the call and drove from the ranch toward Elmore's, grateful Maddox was on top of the search for Tyler. Horseshoe Creek was a huge operation, but the wide-open spaces, land and animals created a homey feeling.

Her father's city estate was large and had never felt like home, whereas the McCullen farmhouse felt warm and welcoming.

Cash looked grim. His mind must be churning with dozens of questions about the case and Tyler, and about the McCullens and the possibility that he was part of that family.

Finding Tyler had to take precedence, though. "Did Sondra mention someplace she'd go if she moved from her father's?"

Cash swung his gaze her way. "She used to talk about the beach, but that was a long time ago."

She changed tactics. "Let's talk about Elmore. Did he have any enemies that you know of?"

Cash removed his hat and ran one hand through his hair. Another scar—this one a cigarette burn on his hand.

She dragged her gaze from it, knowing what it meant. He'd been abused.

An image of a little boy who looked like Cash taunted her. Then an image of a big man pressing a lit cigarette to him to punish him…

"He ticked some other ranchers and employees off, but no one who'd kidnap Tyler, at least not that I can think of," Cash said. "Although, a while back, Sondra mentioned that her father and another rancher had a falling out."

"Did she tell you any details?"

"Just that the man accused her father of cheating him out of a small fortune." He hesitated. "I tried to tell Jasper to look for Elmore's enemies but he blew me off."

"Just tell me what you remember," BJ said softly.

"Not that much. I didn't work for Elmore long at all. In fact, I'd forgotten about that conversation until just now."

"Maybe you forgot, but the rancher didn't." BJ's pulse clamored. "What was his name?"

Cash twisted his mouth to the side as if he

was thinking. “Something like Hicks. No, maybe Nix.”

“I’ll look into it. Anyone else have a beef with him?”

“He fired me, but I wasn’t the first he let go.”

Another leap of her pulse. “A hand who got involved with Sondra?”

“Yeah. A dude named Ronnie made a pass at her a few months back. He was gone the next day.”

“What was his last name?”

“Thacker.”

She made a mental note of his name. “Go on.”

“He accused one of the ranch hands of stealing cattle from him. Threatened to press charges if he didn’t hightail it out of town.”

“So why didn’t he press charges?”

Cash shrugged. “Said he just wanted the trouble to go away.”

“Did you see either man around the ranch after that?”

“No. Although Sondra mentioned that Thacker kept calling her. But that was months ago.”

A possible suspect. "You said Sondra was upset when she called you. Maybe they had a confrontation? He could have followed her, saw you and flew into a rage." Stalkers were obsessive personality types. Their obsessions could become dangerous.

"I suppose. But that seems a stretch."

She sighed. "Cash, work with me here. We have to come up with an alternative suspect if we're going to clear you."

"All right. So the guy drugs me, then kills her and makes me look like the guilty one," Cash said.

It made sense. There was just one problem—the video camera footage of the man who looked like Cash. If he'd been part of a scheme to frame Cash, the killer had planned ahead.

Which meant he hadn't simply flown into a rage and lost control. His anger had built up over time and festered.

That the murder was premeditated.

# *Chapter Eight*

Cash's blood pressure soared as he and BJ walked up the stone drive to Elmore's humongous Georgian home. The man not only had money, but he liked to boast about his good fortune, and showcase it in the details of his home and the furnishings.

Marble floors, custom woodwork, high-end leather couches, custom paintings, and decorated by a designer—there wasn't a space inside that Cash had felt comfortable.

Having grown up in foster care with nothing, at first he'd been irritated at Sondra's comments about growing up in a glass house where she'd been afraid to move or touch anything. But after meeting Elmore and his staff, he'd understood. Sondra had been young, vibrant, and craved love. But she'd felt like a visitor in her own home.

No wonder she hadn't wanted to give up her baby. She was trying to create the family she wanted, not the one she had.

"Should we wait on Maddox?" Cash asked.

BJ shook her head. "Let's talk to Elmore first. If he and Jasper are tight, he may not like idea of another sheriff working the case."

He might even hold back in front of McCullen.

BJ rang the doorbell, and the housekeeper, Ms. Wood, answered with a stiff expression on her gaunt face.

BJ introduced herself. "Mr. Koker and I would like to speak to Mr. Elmore, please."

Disapproval radiated from her pores. "I don't think he wants to see you."

Cash tamped down his anger. He hadn't expected Elmore to welcome him.

"Sheriff McCullen is on his way," BJ said. "You can either let us in now or when he arrives."

The woman cut BJ a sharp look. "Have a seat

in the parlor. I'll inform Mr. Elmore that you're here."

She escorted them to a small room situated off the two-story foyer. BJ rubbed her arms as Ms. Woods disappeared down the hall. "Is it just me or is this place cold?"

Cash grunted. "It's not you. Elmore likes power and social status. He wants everyone to know he has money."

BJ raised her brows, but he quickly clarified his statement. "And no, I didn't resent him for it. I felt sorry for Sondra. Maybe that's why I befriended her. She might have grown up wealthy, but—"

"She grew up poor in other ways," BJ finished.

Cash gave a quick nod. "She never could please her father."

Pain flickered in BJ's eyes for a second. "I can understand that."

"Your father?" Cash asked, surprised.

"My mother died giving birth to me. He shut off his feelings after that."

"You mean he didn't have room to love you?" Cash asked gruffly.

Footsteps echoed from the hallway, and BJ clamped her lips together as Elmore entered the room. He wore a three-piece designer suit and Italian loafers that probably cost a fortune.

Elmore gave Cash a condemning look. "You have nerve showing up at my house, Koker."

"I didn't kill your daughter, Mr. Elmore," Cash said bluntly. "And I certainly didn't kidnap or hurt Tyler. I'm here to help."

"Help?" Elmore said sharply. "I heard my daughter arguing with you on the phone that morning. She said she didn't want to be with you, and you got mad and killed her. Then you took Tyler to get back at me."

"I don't know what you heard, but you have it all wrong." Although they had argued. "That morning when Sondra called me she was upset, but she didn't tell me the reason."

"You're lying to cover for yourself."

"I'm not lying," Cash said. "And for the record, I'm not Tyler's father. Sondra let you believe I was because she didn't want you to know the real father's name."

Elmore's thin face went stone cold. "Of course you'd deny being his parent."

"Listen to me, Elmore, I love that kid. If he was mine, I'd gladly take responsibility for him. Unfortunately, he's not," Cash said.

"We're running Cash's DNA," BJ stated, cutting in. "We'll know soon enough."

"It will prove what I'm saying," Cash said. "Someone set me up, Mr. Elmore. If we work together, maybe we can discover who killed Sondra, and find Tyler."

"Have you heard anything about Tyler?" BJ asked.

Worry creased the man's forehead. "No." He looked at Cash again, his voice earnest. "Listen to me. Just tell me what you want and I'll give it to you. I may not have been the best father, but I want my grandson back."

Cash's chest clenched. "I didn't take him, Mr. Elmore. I swear I didn't."

Elmore paled as if he finally believed him.

"Then who the hell did? And why haven't they contacted me with a ransom demand?"

No one voiced the fear that was hanging over them.

*Because Tyler is dead, too.*

BJ STUDIED ELMORE.

In the case of murder or a child kidnapping, the first place the police usually looked was at the home situation. Family issues or financial problems drove people to do things they might never do. Elmore might appear wealthy on paper, but oftentimes people hid their debts.

The fact that Elmore's relationship with his daughter wasn't perfect raised her suspicions. Had something happened between father and daughter?

"Mr. Elmore, Sheriff McCullen and I reviewed the camera surveillance that allegedly showed Mr. Koker entering the motel where your daughter was killed. The man in the camera footage is not Mr. Koker."

"It sure as hell looked like him!" he said with disbelief. "So what makes you think it wasn't?"

"This," Cash said, pointing to his scar. "The man in the footage didn't have it."

Elmore jerked his head toward Cash, then her. "Then who was it?"

"I was hoping you might have an idea," BJ said.

Anger slashed his features. "How the hell would I know?"

"You might have enemies who want to hurt you. Think about it."

He rubbed his chin with a shaky hand, then poured himself a finger of Scotch and downed it.

"First, though, let's talk about your daughter," BJ continued. "Is there anyone she might have left Tyler with?"

Elmore poured another drink, then swirled it in his highball glass. "Her best friend was from childhood. Diane Stuckey. But Tyler's not with her. I've already checked and Sheriff Jasper checked with her as well."

"Did she talk to Sondra the day Sondra was killed?" BJ asked.

"Diane said she called Sondra, but Sondra didn't answer."

"I'd like to speak to her." BJ would follow up. If Sondra had confided having problems with her father, Diane wouldn't have divulged that to Elmore.

"I'll have my secretary text you her number."

"Thank you." BJ shifted. "We'd also like to look at Sondra's phone and her computer."

"Sheriff Jasper has her phone. He examined her computer and returned it already. It's in her quarters."

The doorbell dinged, and a minute later, the housekeeper escorted Sheriff McCullen and Deputy Whitefeather inside.

Maddox introduced himself and his deputy.

"You're Joe McCullen's oldest, aren't you?" Elmore said.

"Yes, sir."

Elmore shook Maddox's hand. "I'm sorry about your daddy. He was a good man."

Maddox's mouth tightened. "Thank you. I'm also sorry for your loss. I intend to find the person who killed your daughter." He removed an envelope from his pocket. "I have search warrants for your house and for your daughter's living quarters, her phone, car and computer."

A vein pulsed in Elmore's forehead. "You want to search my house? Just what are you looking for?"

Maddox squared his shoulders. "Anything that will lead us to her killer." He gestured toward Cash. "It's possible that Tyler's birth father had motive to take the boy. It's important we find out who he is if you want to bring your grandson home alive."

CASH BRIEFLY ENTERTAINED the idea that Elmore had fought with Sondra and killed her in a fit of rage. But so far the evidence they had uncovered suggested her murder had been premeditated.

Unless Elmore had killed her in the moment, then hired people to frame Cash afterward. He could have paid someone to alter the camera timing and make it appear that "Cash" had been conscious when he'd entered the motel. He could also have paid someone to stage the scene.

Cash tried to envision a scenario of what had happened. If Elmore had argued with Sondra, he would have probably pushed her, not slit her throat with a knife. That type of crime was more violent, implied anger and a cold viciousness.

It just didn't seem likely, any way Cash tried to justify it. Elmore was a rich, snotty son of a bitch who hated Cash, but in spite of their differences, the man had loved his daughter. Slashing his Sondra's throat was too damn bloody for a man like him.

Elmore's hand shook as he gestured to Maddox. "Go ahead and search. More than anything, I want to know who took my daughter and grandson from me."

Cash frowned. Did he know more about Tyler's disappearance than he was letting on? Was he suggesting that Tyler was…dead?

"Is there something you aren't telling us?" Maddox asked. "Do you have any idea who did this, Mr. Elmore?"

Elmore rubbed his forehead with two fingers. “No.” He glanced at Cash. “When Sondra’s friend Diane didn’t have him, I assumed you took Tyler.”

“Mr. Elmore,” Maddox said. “Consider for a second that Cash had nothing to do with this. Think hard about who’d want to hurt Sondra or you.”

Elmore sank into his desk chair. “I’ve had trouble with a few ranchers over the years.” He gave Maddox a pointed look. “Your father and I had our differences, too. But we went by the Cattleman’s code of ethics and were civil enough not to stoop to sabotage. We certainly would never go after each other’s family.”

“Sondra said you accused one of your ranch hands of stealing cattle,” Cash said.

Perspiration beaded on Elmore’s forehead. “Yes, a man named Biff Lenox. It was after your father discovered the cattle-rustling ring. I thought Biff was working with them,” he said to Maddox.

“Did you have proof?” Maddox asked.

"No, or I would have come to you, Sheriff."

"What happened when you confronted him?" Maddox asked.

"He denied it. But he disappeared the next day and never came back." He sighed. "Frankly, I was happy to see him go."

"You put out the word that he was a thief?" Cash asked, remembering the way he'd felt when Elmore had blackballed him.

"I didn't want any of my friends to be taken advantage of," Elmore stated.

"Did you mention this to Jasper?" Maddox asked.

Elmore shrugged. "No, it happened a while back. I didn't think it was connected to Sondra or Tyler."

"I'll look into him," Maddox said. "He might have gotten pissed and come back for revenge."

Elmore stroked one finger over his gold tie clip. "If he hurt Sondra or Tyler, that bastard is going to pay."

"Let me handle it," Maddox said. "My deputy

is going to look around your house. I'd like to see Sondra's living quarters."

"Jasper already went through the house and Sondra's things," Elmore said defensively.

"Just humor me," Maddox said. "He might have missed something."

Elmore motioned toward the hallway. "The guesthouse is out back past the pool."

Deputy Whitefeather headed upstairs to check Sondra's old room and Cash followed Maddox and BJ to the guesthouse.

As soon as they entered and Cash saw Tyler's toys scattered across the den, a pang caught in his chest. Tyler had loved the wooden animals he'd carved for him, especially the horses.

It was hard enough losing Sondra. What if he never got to see Tyler again?

BJ PRESSED A hand to Cash's arm as they stood in the entrance to the guesthouse. "You should stay outside, Cash."

"She's right." Maddox gestured to the patio. "Since you're a suspect, I can't have you inside the victim's home. The DA could argue that you influenced the search. Plus we don't want your fingerprints or DNA on anything here."

Cash's jaw tightened. "I won't touch anything."

"I'm sorry," BJ said. "But Maddox is right. If we find evidence, we don't want the DA or a judge to throw it out because you compromised the scene."

Cash's chiseled jaw went rigid, but he stepped back onto the patio beside the pool.

Maddox moved through the room to search it while BJ did the same. She checked the kitchen while he examined the desk in the den. Two used wineglasses sat on the counter, suggesting that someone had joined Sondra for a drink the day she died. Unless she made a habit of leaving dirty dishes for days?

"If Jasper searched in here why didn't he send those to the lab?"

"Good question." Maddox bagged them. "I'll check with Jasper to see if his people found prints or DNA."

BJ peeked inside the dishwasher. Half-full. The

cabinets were neat and orderly, the pantry filled with kid's cereal, a box of macaroni and cheese, Goldfish, pudding cups, and a stack of energy bars that she assumed were Sondra's.

The fridge held a carton of milk, yogurt, various cheeses, orange juice, salad fixings, condiments, hot dogs and a leftover pizza box with two slices of cheese pizza.

Silverware and kitchen utensils were in the drawers. A box of matches from a honky-tonk named Cowgirls. Receipts for clothing at a women's boutique. A bill from a martial arts studio for lessons for Tyler.

BJ hoped to find a day calendar or journal, something to provide information about what Sondra had been doing the day she died, or about Tyler's father. No luck.

Maddox looked up from the desk. "Nothing in here. I'll search the bedroom."

A cookie jar shaped like a bear stood on top of the refrigerator. If Sondra wanted to hide something, it was the perfect spot.

BJ grabbed a paper towel so as not to contaminate it with her fingerprints, rose on her tiptoes and pulled it down, then dug inside. Disappointment filled her when she found chocolate chip cookies, but nothing else.

Frustrated, she stepped into the bedroom. Maddox had donned plastic gloves and was searching the dresser, so she went to the closet, a walk-in that held more clothes than BJ had owned in her entire lifetime.

Although she expected expensive ball gowns, designer shoes and purses—and there were a few of them—most of the items were casual clothes, jeans, sweaters and T-shirts she probably wore to play with her son. BJ dug in the pockets of the woman's coats. A pair of gloves and lip gloss.

"I found her computer," Maddox said as he booted it up. "Now I need her password."

"I'll ask Cash and see if he knows." She stepped outside. "Cash, do you have any idea what Sondra's password is?"

He frowned. "Her birthday? No, wait, try Tyler's birthday."

That made sense. "What is the date?"

"June 5."

BJ rushed back to Maddox and gave him the information.

Maddox typed the date. "That's it. Thanks."

"I'll look in Tyler's room." BJ crossed the hall. Her heart melted at the sight of the little boy's sports-themed comforter and the assortment of trucks, cars and building blocks.

A set of what looked like hand-carved horses and farm animals stood on a shelf as if they were special.

She pressed her hand to her chest, her heart aching as an image of her son flashed back. She could see him building a castle with those blocks. Drawing a picture of the horse he wanted one day.

Tears blurred her vision, but she swiped at them and forced her feet to move forward. Sometimes the painful memories brought her to her knees.

But she had work to do. Tyler's life might depend on them getting answers fast.

Using a small towel to cover her hands, she searched the little boy's toy chest and dresser, then opened his closet. On the top shelf, several shoeboxes filled with toys were lined up.

She discovered another box in the corner, and she pulled it down and opened it.

Her pulse picked up. Two envelopes were tucked inside. She opened the first one and found Tyler's birth certificate. Hope spiked. Surely Sondra had listed the boy's father on the paper.

BJ flipped it open and gaped at the name listed as Tyler's father.

Cash Koker.

# *Chapter Nine*

Cash paced outside the guesthouse. He felt helpless and useless and he damn well didn't like it.

If someone had planted evidence against him, no telling what BJ and Maddox might find in Sondra's place.

He racked his brain to remember if Sondra had mentioned any particular man other than Ronnie who'd expressed an interest in her. But no one came to mind. Although she was young and attractive. There *had* to be somebody.

He should have pushed her to tell him what was wrong over the phone that night.

But he thought they'd have time.

BJ stepped from the guesthouse, her expression

solemn. Suspicious again. Maddox followed, his jaw set.

Cash's stomach clenched. "Did you find something?"

Maddox cleared his throat. "Sondra's computer. But someone erased content. I'll talk to Jasper and see if he found anything, then I'll see if the lab can recover what was deleted."

BJ was holding an envelope. "I found Tyler's birth certificate tucked in a shoebox in Tyler's closet."

"So she listed Tyler's father," Cash said with a burst of hope.

BJ met his gaze with troubled eyes, then gestured toward the paper. "She listed you as Tyler's father, Cash."

His breath stalled in his chest. Dammit to hell. She'd been serious about keeping the father's identity a secret.

BJ WANTED TO believe Cash, but this birth certificate made it difficult. "You said you weren't Tyler's father."

"I'm not," Cash said.

Maddox examined the document. "Then why did Sondra Elmore list you as the baby's daddy?"

Cash rubbed the back of his neck. "I honestly don't know. I figured she left the father's name blank. Maybe she wanted me to have ties to Tyler in some way, but the DNA will prove the truth of the matter.

"That would explain why everyone is so adamant that Tyler is your child," Maddox observed. "I don't think I need to guess Elmore's reaction to the whole thing."

Cash stretched his hands in front of him and stared at his blunt nails. Scars crisscrossed his skin and one finger was completely crooked, as if it had been broken and never been treated. More burn marks stood out, cigarette burns that revealed more about his past.

"I wasn't good enough for Sondra," Cash said. "It's not like I have a pedigree. I was a ranch hand. I had no idea who my parents were." He grunted. "Not exactly what Elmore wanted in a son-in-law. He wanted someone who fit into society, someone to show off to his friends."

"Sounds like the way Dad described Elmore," Maddox said.

Was Cash Joe McCullen's son, as well?

Maddox stowed Sondra's computer in his SUV. "Cash, tell me about the argument you and Sondra had the day she died."

BJ stiffened, hoping Cash had a good answer. So far, things kept stacking up against him.

Cash lifted his chin, his jaw hard. "Yes, we argued, but it's not what you think. I suggested she ask Jasper to issue a restraining order against this guy Ronnie, but she said she couldn't talk to Jasper."

"Did she say why?" Maddox asked.

Cash shook his head. "Apparently Jasper's father and Elmore were friends. She didn't want her father to worry."

"It seems odd that Jasper and Elmore are friends," Maddox said. "The age difference is significant. Plus Jasper isn't a rancher."

"Apparently, back in the day, Jasper's father and Elmore were roommates at some elitist boarding school," Cash said.

Maddox made a low sound beneath his breath. "I see. So Elmore could have the sheriff in his pocket."

"That would explain a lot," BJ said. "Did Elmore have financial problems?" she asked Cash.

Cash rolled his eyes. "If he had money trouble, he certainly didn't tell me about it."

"What about Sondra?" Maddox asked. "I assume he supported her and Tyler financially?"

"Yes. She received a monthly allowance."

"If she was rebellious and her father was controlling, why didn't she try to get a job and move out on her own?"

Cash shifted. "I wondered that, too. When I first met her, she was in college, said she wanted to study journalism. But when she got pregnant, she changed."

"How so?" Maddox asked.

"She dropped out of school. Started staying

home more. At first she even seemed withdrawn." He worked his mouth from side to side. "I asked her if something was wrong, but she claimed she was just tired."

BJ raised a brow. "You said she and her father argued—maybe he told her he was cutting back that allowance."

"I guess it's possible," Cash said. "Sondra depended on that money for her and Tyler to live."

"Did the baby's father contribute financially?" Maddox asked with a frown.

Cash shook his head. "She said she didn't want anything from him."

BJ made a disapproving sound. "She could have been frightened of him."

Maddox removed his hat and scraped a hand through his dark hair, then settled his Stetson back on his head. "Do you think it's possible that this guy took advantage of her, Cash? That they weren't romantically involved?"

Cash jerked his head up, his eyes cold. "You mean do I think he raped her?"

CASH HAD NEVER considered that possibility. But it would explain the reason she seemed afraid to talk about Tyler's father. And also the reason she didn't want to disclose his identity or care that he wasn't in her and Tyler's life.

If Elmore thought a man had forced himself on Sondra, he would kill him.

Cash would kill him, too.

But surely Sondra would have told him if she'd been attacked.

Wouldn't she?

Unless…she'd been a victim of date rape. She'd always said it was her fault she'd gotten pregnant, that she'd been stupid and irresponsible…

He'd assumed she meant that she simply hadn't used birth control.

Maybe Whitefeather would find something inside Elmore's house.

"Cash?" BJ said with an eyebrow raise.

"I…don't know," he said honestly. "It would explain why she refused to talk about him. And the reason she was so upset when she first discovered the pregnancy."

"Also the reason she didn't move out," BJ added. "Perhaps she didn't feel safe."

"Did you ever see bruises on her?" Maddox asked.

Cash struggled to recall the past three years. "A couple of times, maybe. Once I touched her shoulder and she reacted in pain, but she said she'd taken a fall off a horse."

"You think her father hit her?" BJ asked.

Cash's mind raced to comments between the father and daughter. He'd heard raised voices, and Sondra had been in tears a few times. "Elmore threatened to disown her when he learned about the pregnancy. But I don't think he hit her. And in the end, he gave her the guesthouse and supported her, although he spent very little time with Tyler."

"So if she wasn't afraid of her father, she was afraid of Tyler's daddy," BJ said.

Cash balled his hands into fists. He'd tried to respect her privacy by not pushing her too much for the man's name.

She might still be alive if he had.

BJ HATED THE train of thought her mind had taken. But they had to consider all the possibilities.

Elmore was a proud, astute man who valued his place in society, just like her own father.

How would her dad react if she'd turned up pregnant and decided to stay single?

He would be livid. He would have suggested a quiet abortion. He might have even cut her out of his life.

Just telling him would have made BJ ill.

Had Sondra felt that way?

Still, Tyler was an innocent little boy. How could Elmore not have loved that child?

Deputy Whitefeather appeared from the house, carrying a box.

"Did you find something?" Maddox asked.

The deputy gave a quick nod. "A few pictures of Sondra with a couple of different men. Thought one of them might be Tyler's father."

"Their names?" BJ asked.

"Not on the pics, but the lab can run them through facial recognition."

"Good idea," Maddox said. "Anything else?"

"Some notebooks, journals that belong to Sondra. I haven't gone through them, but they seem personal."

"Let me examine them," BJ said. "Maybe she talks about the baby's daddy in there."

Maddox and the deputy agreed, and they walked to their vehicles together. Maddox's phone buzzed and he stepped aside to answer it. Worry knitted his brow as he hung up. "Elmore agreed to let me put a trace on his phone in case of a ransom call."

Whitefeather stepped up. "I'll take the computer and pictures to the lab. I'll also check Elmore's bank accounts and financials. If he's in trouble, and had an insurance policy on his daughter and/or grandson, that would be motive."

"Keep me informed," BJ said. "Just put the box in my car."

"Could I see the pictures?" Cash asked. "Maybe I'll recognize one of the men."

"Sure," Maddox said. "But let's do it at the

sheriff's office. I don't want any question over proper procedure or chain of custody."

Whitefeather stowed the box in the backseat of BJ's sedan.

BJ and Cash followed Deputy Whitefeather to the sheriff's office, where he left the box in an interrogation room. Cash shifted as if he was growing antsier by the minute.

BJ spread the pictures across the table before they tackled the notebooks.

There were several candids of Sondra and Tyler at the park. Others depicted them riding horses, celebrating the little boy's birthday and Christmases. Sondra was smiling and obviously doted on her son.

Oddly, there were no pictures of Tyler and his grandfather.

She shuffled further and found photos of Sondra and two different men. One was a tall, fair-haired cowboy who was standing close to her in one of the stables.

"Do you recognize him?" BJ asked.

Cash studied the photograph. "Mike Cranford. He works for Elmore."

"Were he and Sondra involved?"

"No. The man's gay."

Hmm. Another picture revealed a shorter, stockier guy with reddish hair leaning in for a kiss. "How about him?"

"No clue," Cash said.

BJ listened for jealousy in his voice but detected none.

Cash thumped his boot on the floor. "I wonder who took these pictures."

BJ drummed her fingers on the table. "Good point."

"What if Ronnie Thacker was following her and he took them?"

"That's a possibility," BJ said, her mind racing. "If she was romantic with one of these men, Ronnie could have been jealous. But if he took them, why did Sondra have them?"

"Maybe he sent them to her. And that's the reason she thought he was stalking her?"

"Another good point." A possible scenario

flashed in BJ's mind's eye—of Sondra confronting Ronnie. Ronnie became upset, lost control and killed her.

Then in desperation, he'd come up with a plan to frame Cash.

CASH FELT LIKE he was invading Sondra's privacy as he and BJ combed through his friend's notebooks.

"Look for dates, references to men, to Ronnie, to any arguments with her father or anyone else," BJ said. "If this is about Elmore, she may have heard something, an altercation between him and another rancher or person who wanted to hurt him."

The lab tech texted with an address for Thacker. Biff Lenox, the man Elmore accused of working with the cattle-rustling ring, had disappeared.

"Let's go," BJ said.

Cash checked his watch as they drove to Thacker's. Dammit, he wanted to find Tyler before nightfall.

"You should wait in the car," BJ said as they approached the farm.

"No way." Cash folded his arms. "I want Thacker to look into my eyes and tell me he didn't hurt Sondra or Tyler."

A debate settled in BJ's eyes, but finally she conceded. "All right, but if you don't control yourself, Cash, it'll be the last time I allow you to go with me. If it's necessary, I'll have Maddox lock you back up."

A dozen curse words rattled in Cash's head, but he bit them back. He didn't play by the rules. He never had. But at least BJ was on his side. He couldn't afford to lose that help.

Farm and ranch lands spread for miles, signs of summer evident in the blazing sun, and how the lack of rain was frying the grass. Her SUV bounced over the uneven terrain.

A second later, BJ made a turn onto a long dirt road, but just as she did, a gunshot rang out. BJ screamed and swerved to the left. Cash jerked his head around to see where the shot was coming from and spotted a black pickup barreling on their tail.

Another gunshot pierced the back window. "Duck!" Cash yelled.

BJ dropped her head as low as possible and cut to the right, but another gunshot sounded. The bullet must have hit the tire because it blew, the sedan swerved out of control and they careened toward a boulder at the edge of the ridge.

Cash saw the drop off approaching and realized they weren't going to stop in time. "Jump, BJ!"

Her eyes widened in panic. She was clearly too frightened to propel herself from the moving vehicle. He whipped his seat belt off, then hers, grabbed her hand and threw open the door.

He dragged her across the seat and yanked her out of the car with him. He wrapped his arms around her to protect her and took the brunt of the fall. Gravel, pavement and dirt clawed at him, and he rolled them toward the grassy roadside.

A second later, BJ's car slid over the edge.

# *Chapter Ten*

Terror streaked through BJ as Cash dragged her from the car, wrapped his body around hers and rolled away from the ravine. The impact jarred her shoulder; gravel scraped her cheek and hands. A bullet zinged by her head.

"Stay down!" Cash shouted.

The weight of his body felt warm and comforting, yet whoever was shooting at them was still firing.

Cash's breath gushed out as he lifted his head and scanned the area. BJ's car had skidded to the edge and was hanging by a thread over the side.

"Crawl behind that bush," Cash whispered next to her ear.

Footsteps crunched gravel. Terrified, BJ scooted toward the bushes. Cash slid his hand inside his jacket, removed a pistol and fired back at the man. Shock bolted through BJ. When had Cash gotten hold of a gun?

She didn't have time to analyze the fact that he was violating the law because the shooter fired again. She hid in the bushes and tried to get a look at his face, but his hat sat so low on his head that it was impossible to see his eyes or even his hair color.

Cash released a round, and a curse rent the air as the bullet pinged on the ground near the man's foot.

Their assailant fired into the bushes, and she scampered to the right and crouched behind a tree.

Cash moved quietly, sneaking up on the man. More noise suggested the shooter had pivoted and was stalking toward them.

A grunt followed. Cash attacking the man.

He grabbed the guys' legs and dragged him down to the ground. They rolled and fought for the gun. It went off again, this bullet hitting a tree branch and sending leaves raining down.

Cash punched the shooter with his fist. Blood spurted from his nose and the gun flew out of his hand. BJ eyed the distance to it, but the man kicked Cash in the face and scampered toward it. His fingers touched the handle just as Cash reached him. Cash launched himself on top of him, flipped him over and slammed his fist into the man's face once more.

The shooter bellowed, but managed to lift the gun and shove it in Cash's chest.

BJ lost her breath. Cash grappled for the weapon and rolled, fighting and punching.

Just as they neared the edge, the gun went off again.

CASH HEAVED A breath as the gunman fell over the edge. The man clawed the embankment, struggling to keep from falling below. A bullet had grazed Cash's shoulder, and he tasted dirt as he looked into the man's eyes.

An expression of cold evil glinted back. "You gonna kill me by pushing me over?"

Cash was tempted. But he wanted answers instead.

A dead man couldn't talk.

The sound of BJ's car crashing to the bottom of the ravine rent the air. Dammit. They would have been in that car.

Cash grabbed the gunman's hand and tried to pull him back up.

The man's hat flew off, sailing to the bottom of the ravine just as BJ's car had. He felt like dead weight as Cash hauled him to safety. The man groaned and fell onto the grass, his breath rasping.

A second later, he punched Cash and grabbed the gun again.

Cash cursed and rolled sideways to avoid the bullet. The man lunged toward him again. Cash kicked him hard in the chest and sent him careening backward. His attacker's foot hit a loose rock, more rocks skittered down the embankment and the man flailed his arms to keep upright.

He failed, bellowing as he plunged below.

Cash crawled to the edge, his breathing ragged, and stared into the ravine. BJ jumped up from her hiding place, raced to him and dropped to her knees. The man's body lay twisted and mangled on the jagged rocks.

She gently laid a hand on Cash's back. "Are you hurt?"

Anger shot through him. "No, but dammit, he's dead."

Her gaze searched his. "Do you recognize him?"

"Never seen the bastard before."

"So that isn't Ronnie?"

Cash shook his head. "No. But I intend to find out who he is."

And why he wanted them dead. Or at least why he wanted *him* dead.

Things had just gone from bad to worse. If Sheriff Jasper got hold of this news, he'd use it as an excuse to lock Cash's butt back up and throw away the key. Even if BJ backed up his story, Jasper would do everything he could to make Cash's life hell until the truth came out.

*If* the truth came out. Someone was clearly trying to frame him for murder. There was no telling what lengths they'd go to. And he didn't want BJ hurt.

"My purse was in the car, but I've got my phone," BJ said. "I'll call for help."

"I'll check out his vehicle," Cash said. "Maybe his ID is inside. We can also try to run his plates."

BJ caught his arm. "Don't touch anything, Cash. Remember you're the primary suspect in a murder investigation."

Cash cursed beneath his breath. How could he help himself if he had to sit back and twiddle his damn thumbs?

"Maddox will help us," BJ said softly.

His stomach somersaulted at the concern in her eyes. How long had it been since a woman had cared about him?

*She doesn't care, Cash. She's your lawyer. Hell, if she decides you're guilty, she'll call the cops on you herself.*

"Are you sure you don't need a doctor?" she asked.

Cash swallowed hard. "Trust me, I've had worse." From foster fathers with a hard hand.

Sympathy filled her eyes as if she'd read his mind.

By God, the last thing in the world he wanted from her was pity.

He yanked a handkerchief from his pocket and dabbed at the blood to prove the wound wasn't serious. "See, it just grazed the skin."

Her hand trembled as she punched in Maddox's number. She obviously didn't get shot at every day. He'd had enough scrapes and beatings in his life to blow this one off without a second thought.

Despair threatened to choke Cash. What if he'd killed the only person who knew Tyler's whereabouts, and Tyler was someplace alone, hungry and cold? And so far off the grid no one would ever find him?

That thought made Cash want to double over in rage.

But he couldn't waste time. He needed answers.

Desperate, he picked himself up, retrieved his gun and stowed it in his jacket. Then he rushed to the dead man's car. Hopefully, he'd find something inside that would lead him to the truth.

BJ READ THE frustration on Cash's face. He'd hidden his gun in his jacket, but she decided not to mention it.

The only way to help him was to get answers.

She phoned Maddox and explained the situation.

"My deputy will be there ASAP," Maddox said, then he hung up.

She raced to the shooter's truck. Cash had the door open and was searching the interior.

She looked over his shoulder. A box of ammunition on the seat. A rifle lay on the floorboard—the weapon the gunman had used to shoot at her car. He'd also had a pistol. He'd pulled it from his back pocket and used it to fire at Cash.

She snapped pictures with her phone, then opened the dash and found more shells. No wallet. He probably had it on him.

"I'll look in the truck bed," Cash said.

She started to argue, but if this man had stashed Tyler somewhere, the little boy's life depended on them acting quickly.

Cash rushed to the back while she checked the vehicle registration. She found proof of insurance, a hunting and fishing license, and a burner phone.

The truck was registered to a man named Taft Rumkin. The other documents were registered under the same name.

"Anything in the truck bed?" she asked.

Cash lifted his head, a weary look in his eyes. "No. No sign of Tyler."

A siren wailed, and Deputy Whitefeather sped up in his police-issued SUV. A tow truck and crew, along with a crime scene unit from the county, careened to a stop behind him.

A flurry of motion ensued as the workers exited their vehicles and joined the deputy.

She'd done her homework on the deputy sheriff. Apparently Joe McCullen had been romantically involved with Whitefeather's mother before he married the woman who'd given birth to the McCullen brothers—and possibly Cash. That made Whitefeather a half brother.

He'd also spearheaded the investigation into Joe's death and had uncovered the fact that Joe McCullen's wife had been murdered and the twins kidnapped.

The head of the towing company and his men began to assess the situation and develop a plan to extricate her car. Two of the CSI team members harnessed up to climb down, photograph and process the body, and bring it up.

BJ carried Rumkin's documents to the deputy. "The man driving that pickup shot at us and tried to kill Cash. According to the vehicle registration, his name is Taft Rumkin."

The sun glinted off Deputy Whitefeather's dark skin as he turned to Cash. "Did you know him?"

"No, never heard of him." Cash swiped at a bead of sweat on his forehead. "We had to jump from the car or we'd have gone over that ridge with BJ's sedan."

Deputy Whitefeather scowled, then glanced

down at BJ's demolished car. He whistled at the distance. "Looks like he ended up there, too. What happened?"

"I lost control," BJ said. "Cash pulled me from the car and saved my life."

The deputy's eyes focused on Cash. "That true?"

Cash simply shrugged, then jammed his hands in his back pockets.

"The man kept shooting," BJ continued. "We rolled into the bushes, and I hid behind a tree while Cash snuck up on him." She paused, her breath heaving as her adrenaline waned. "Cash and the man fought. The man lost his balance and fell over the edge."

"You push him?" Deputy Whitefeather asked Cash.

BJ cleared her throat. "That's not the way it happened. Cash actually dragged him up over the edge to save him, but he attacked Cash again. If Cash hadn't defended us, we'd both be dead."

The wind swirled the smoke still rising from

BJ's vehicle below as the gravity of the situation sank in.

Cash was innocent. Tyler was still missing.

And someone didn't want them asking questions or poking around. Someone who'd kill to keep them from finding the truth.

# *Chapter Eleven*

BJ shivered at the sight of her crushed vehicle as Deputy Whitefeather and the crime team worked.

If Cash hadn't dragged her from the car, she'd be dead. "Someone is nervous that we're asking questions about Sondra's death and about Tyler."

Cash murmured agreement, his face a solemn mask. She could almost feel the anger building inside him. He was a tough, huge man, with muscles strong enough to tear up a rock.

What would happen if he unleashed his frustration? According to his rap sheet, he had a couple arrests for bar brawls.

"I'm sorry about your car," he said quietly.

BJ's jittery nerves settled slightly. "It's insured. I'll get a rental until I replace it."

"We can use my truck," Cash offered. "It's not as nice as your car, but it runs."

The realization that he had little money and Elmore had treated him as if he was lesser because of it roused BJ's temper. "Cash, we need transportation. It doesn't matter what kind of vehicle it is. I'll call the McCullens and ask one of them to bring your truck."

He nodded, but the uncertainty in his eyes endeared him to her even more. What would it take for Cash to learn to trust someone?

"THE MCCULLENS ARE good people," Deputy Whitefeather said. "You can trust them. They accepted me."

Cash narrowed his eyes. "You're related to them?"

Deputy Whitefeather nodded. "Half brother."

Which meant that if Cash was a McCullen, the deputy was his half brother, as well.

Late afternoon shadows painted the skies a

murky gray as the crew finished hauling BJ's car from the ravine. The medical examiner arrived along with an ambulance, and he examined Rumkin's body.

Cash studied the dead man's face for recognition, but nothing clicked.

The ME looked up from Rumkin's body. "Cause of death was head trauma from the fall."

Deputy Whitefeather knelt beside the ME and checked the man's hands. "Powder burns confirm that he fired the weapon."

The crime team collected bullet casings and retrieved the gun he'd fired at Cash. Another investigator dug two bullets from BJ's car. So far everything supported his and BJ's statements.

Brett arrived in Cash's pickup truck, with one of the ranch hands following. "Gosh, you guys were lucky," he said as he peered over the ridge.

"Cash's quick thinking saved us," BJ said.

Brett met his gaze, making Cash fidget. The McCullens were dissecting every movement and word he said. Even if he was related to them, which was still a big if, they didn't have to call him a McCullen.

Elmore had talked about how close-knit the family was, that although they'd had problems, they stuck together.

He couldn't imagine that kind of loyalty.

"Thanks for bringing my truck." He turned to BJ. "Maybe you should let me look into this on my own. Being with me is putting you in danger."

"There's no way I'm walking away," BJ said. "Besides, you're the one who shouldn't be involved in the investigation."

The sound of BJ's scream as he'd jerked her from the car taunted Cash. "I just don't want you to be hurt because of me."

"Don't worry about me. This is not the first case I've worked that got rough." She took her purse from one of the CSIs and thanked him for retrieving it. "I want to talk to Ronnie Thacker tonight."

Deputy Whitefeather made a clicking sound

with his teeth. "I'll go with you two. The judge or DA can't argue with that."

The deputy stowed the box of Sondra's notebooks in Cash's truck, then Cash and BJ followed Whitefeather along the farm road to Thacker's. The deputy eased into the drive and Cash parked behind him.

The property was run-down, the pastures overgrown, farm equipment rusty and broken. A dilapidated barn tilted at an odd angle, as if it was sinking into the ground. Vultures soared near a dried-up creek.

They climbed from their vehicles and strode up the graveled drive. Whitefeather knocked on the door, but the hair on the back of Cash's neck bristled.

He pivoted, braced for trouble. Ronnie Thacker stood by a giant oak near the barn with a rifle pointed at them.

BJ FROZE AT the sight of the rifle. Cash instantly pushed her behind him. "Don't move, BJ."

Deputy Whitefeather's hand slid to his gun. "Listen, Mr. Thacker, put down the rifle. We only want to talk. No one needs to get hurt."

"You're the law. That mean I'm in trouble?" Thacker shouted.

"Not if you haven't done anything wrong," Whitefeather said calmly.

BJ pressed one hand to Cash's back. She could practically feel his heart pounding. She and Cash had escaped death once today. She didn't intend to push their luck.

Thacker aimed the rifle toward Cash. "What are you doing on my land?"

"We need to talk to you about Sondra and Tyler Elmore," BJ said.

Thacker tilted his hat backward, revealing bushy eyebrows and sweat streaking his face. But he kept the gun trained on Cash. "You here to gloat and tell me the two of you are getting hitched?"

Cash glanced at the deputy, then BJ. Was Thacker pretending innocence or did he really not know about Sondra and Tyler?

BJ gave a little shrug, silently urging Cash to play along. If the man was lying, they'd find out soon enough.

"Sondra and I were just friends," Cash said.

Whitefeather gestured toward the rifle. "Nothing can come of shooting anyone," he said. "So put the gun down."

Thacker spewed a litany of curse words, then slowly lowered the weapon. "All right. But someone better start talking or else get the hell off of my property."

"You liked Sondra," BJ said, taking the lead. Hopefully, Thacker would open up more to a female. The man had been eyeing her with appreciation. "Were you dating?"

Thacker shrugged. "We were. At least I thought so, then she got all weird and stopped answering my calls."

"When did you last see her or talk to her?" Deputy Whitefeather asked.

Thacker grunted. "Last week. Why?"

Cash tensed, but BJ gently placed a hand on

his arm. "Did you see her or talk on the phone?" she asked.

The man glanced down at his boots with a sour expression. "She was in town at the honky-tonk."

"Really?" BJ asked. "Were you two hanging out?"

Thacker cut his eyes toward the pasture. "No, she took out this stupid restraining order, so I stayed on the other side of the room. She was flirting with some cowboy."

"You didn't talk to her?" BJ asked.

He shook his head. "No. I…didn't want to bother them."

"You mean you didn't want to violate the restraining order," Deputy Whitefeather said.

Thacker's shoulders drew back defensively.

"Who was Sondra talking to?" Cash asked.

Thacker hissed. "I don't know the jerk's name, but he wasn't good enough for her."

"But you were?" BJ said.

Thacker shuffled onto the balls of his feet. "I love her. Now, why you asking me all these questions?"

BJ traded looks with Cash and the deputy. "Because Sondra Elmore was murdered Friday night."

Thacker's face paled, and he staggered sideways. "No… Sondra can't be dead…she can't be."

He dropped his head into his hands and moaned. "She and I were going to get married one day. Have a family." He waved his hand, gesturing to the farm. "I was going to fix this place up, show her I could be somebody."

"Maybe you told her that, and she said she could never love you, so you killed her," BJ suggested.

"No!" Thacker lunged toward her and grabbed her arm.

BJ gripped his hands with her fingers to loosen his hold.

A second later, Cash grabbed Thacker by the collar and slammed him against the wall of the house.

CASH SHOOK THE BASTARD. "Sondra called me to meet her. She was upset, but she wouldn't tell me the reason. Said she had to see me in person.

It was because she was afraid of you." His voice cracked. "You were stalking her," Cash continued. "You couldn't stand that she didn't want you, so you finally lost it and got revenge."

The man trembled. "That's not the way it happened."

Cash tightened his grip. BJ murmured something in the background, urging him to release Thacker.

Whitefeather moved up behind him. "Cash, take it easy."

"Then how did it happen?" Cash barked.

"I didn't hurt Sondra," Thacker cried. "I loved her. I would never have done anything to harm her." Tears leaked from his eyes. "I had a plan. After she filed that damned restraining order, the judge talked to me and I signed up for anger management classes."

Cash kept his fingers clenched around the man's collar. "So you went to tell her, but it wasn't enough. You realized nothing you did would ever be enough. Maybe she threatened to call the police."

“No.” Thacker pried Cash’s fingers from his neck. “I did see her at that bar, but I didn’t talk to her. I wanted to prove to her I was changing, so I left.”

“Anybody leave with you?” BJ asked.

Thacker cursed. “No.”

“Then what did you do?” Cash growled.

Thacker scraped a shaky hand over his face. “I went driving around and then went skeet shooting to blow off some steam.”

“Is that all you were shooting?” Cash asked.

“Y-yes,” Thacker stammered.

“Where did you go shooting?” Deputy Whitefeather asked.

Thacker wiped sweat from his neck. “To the pond on the north side of my property. My daddy set up a little fishing camp there years ago. That’s always where we went to shoot.”

“Can anyone corroborate your story?”

Fear streaked Thacker’s face. “No. I…I was alone.”

Cash couldn’t stand the tension another minute. Tyler’s life might be hanging in the balance, and

Whitefeather was beating around the bush, probably worried about violating the bastard's rights.

No one had given a damn about his rights when Jasper threw him in a holding cell and refused to let him call anyone for two days. "Is Tyler out at that fishing camp?"

Thacker stumbled backward, his mouth agape. "What do you mean? Why would Tyler be here?"

"Whoever murdered Sondra took Tyler." Cash's agitation mounted. "You'd better not have hurt him, Thacker. Now take us to him."

"I didn't take the kid." Thacker looked panicked. "That's the God-honest truth."

"Then you won't mind if we search your property?" Deputy Whitefeather said.

Thacker sucked in a sharp breath, then glanced from one of them to the other, worry darkening his eyes. "You're serious? Sondra's little boy is missing?"

"Yes," BJ said. "He may be in danger. So if you know where he is, tell us. The DA will go a lot easier on you if we find Tyler alive."

# *Chapter Twelve*

BJ studied Thacker. He was shaking in his shoes.

Because he was innocent or guilty?

He seemed sincerely shocked that Sondra was dead and that Tyler was missing.

*You've been wrong before.*

"You can look around all you want," Thacker said. "Sondra's son isn't here."

"Did you take him somewhere else?" Cash asked.

"I told you, I didn't kidnap that kid." Ronnie scraped a hand through his shaggy, unkempt hair. "Why would I take the boy? I wanted Sondra, not him."

Cash gave him a cold look. "Maybe you killed

Sondra in a fit of passion, but the boy was there and you had to do something, get rid of him."

"You're crazy," Thacker said.

Cash ignored the man's barb. "Then you had the boy and decided to use him to extract some cash out of Elmore." Cash gestured at the run-down farm equipment parked by the dilapidated barn. "Looks like you need some updates around here."

Ronnie shook his head vehemently. "I wanted to fix the place up to impress Sondra. If she's gone, I've got no incentive."

"IF YOU'RE INNOCENT, let us look around inside," BJ said.

Thacker scowled "Don't you need a warrant?"

"You want me to get a warrant," the deputy said. "Makes it sound like you're hiding something."

Ronnie gripped his hands together. "I ain't hiding nothing."

Deputy Whitefeather tossed BJ a pair of latex

gloves. "Koker, wait outside and don't touch anything, you hear me?"

Cash silently cursed. He wanted to do something, dammit. He'd never in his life left his fate to strangers.

*BJ is defending you,* he reminded himself. *And the deputy may be your half brother.*

If he couldn't trust them, he couldn't trust anyone.

Still, he didn't like depending on anyone else. Or owing them.

Whitefeather hooked a thumb toward his SUV. "Take me to the pond where you went skeet shooting."

BJ disappeared inside the house, and Cash leaned against his truck, images of Tyler haunting him as the deputy drove across the farm with Thacker.

"Where are you, Tyler?" Was he safe? Hurt? Terrified?

Did he know that his mother was gone?

A sick feeling welled in Cash's gut as another possibility occurred to him.

Tyler had been with Sondra the night she'd called him in a panic. He'd heard the little boy's voice in the background.

He hadn't come into the bar with her, but what if she'd locked him in the car? That would explain why she'd been in such a hurry to go outside to talk.

Cash's anxiety mounted. What if Tyler hadn't been kidnapped for a ransom? What if he'd witnessed his mother's murder and the killer took him to prevent Tyler from talking?

BJ KEPT HER senses alert as she entered Thacker's house. She didn't know exactly what she was looking for, a toy or kid's blanket—anything, that might indicate a child had been in the house.

Or that Thacker had kept something of Sondra's—a souvenir of some sort.

His history of stalking, the restraining order against him, plus the fact that he was at the bar the night Sondra was killed and had no alibi all made him a viable alternative suspect to

Cash, at least enough to cast reasonable doubt on Cash's guilt.

She scanned the entryway. A coat rack with a denim jacket draped over it. Muddy work boots on the floor. She had a clear sight into the den, which held a faded brown plaid couch and a leather recliner. A deer head hung over the mantel. Dark hues and paneling made the place feel masculine, but the threadbare curtains and pillows gave it a dated feel.

No signs a female had been inside. BJ dug through the desk looking for motel receipts indicating that he'd booked a room at the motel where Sondra had been murdered, but the only paperwork she found were past-due bills.

She moved to the kitchen next. The outdated linoleum was ripped, and the cabinets desperately needed painting. A chipped pine table held empty coffee cups and dirty dishes along with takeout bags. The refrigerator held a carton of milk, eggs, stale bread and leftovers. No kids' cereal or juice or any sign that Tyler had been here.

She examined the pantry and coat closet, then moved to the extra bedroom. An ancient iron bed with a faded throw and tattered carpet. Nothing suspicious.

Next she scoped out Thacker's bedroom. An oak bed with a rustic quilt, brown armchair, curtains hanging askew. Again, no signs of a female or a child.

Thacker had supposedly stalked Sondra, though.

Stalkers were obsessive; they fed their fantasies by keeping photographs or objects belonging to the people they were infatuated with.

She searched Thacker's dresser drawers. Nothing female inside.

Still not satisfied, she dropped to her knees and peered under Thacker's bed.

A boot box.

Her interest spiked, she pulled it out and lifted the top. There were dozens of pictures of Sondra inside.

Candid shots of Sondra in town, exiting a restaurant, entering a store, at the park with Tyler, riding on the ranch with Tyler.

A cold chill rippled up BJ's spine.

In the pictures, Sondra looked beautiful with the sun glinting off her sun-kissed skin and hair. The love and adoration for her son brought tears to BJ's eyes.

A mother and son's bond was special.

If Tyler was alive and they found him, he would grow up without his mother.

That fact alone hardened her resolve to find the truth.

CASH SCANNED THE property for a place Thacker could hide Tyler. He strode around the outside of the house in search of a crawl space, root cellar or emergency underground fallout shelter, but found nothing.

Damn.

A dilapidated barn that looked as if it was sinking into the ground sat to the right. He started toward it, but BJ shouted his name just as he reached for the wooden door.

"Cash, I told you not to touch anything."

He kicked the dirt at his feet, but stepped to the

side. “I haven’t touched anything. But we should give this place a look.”

She blew out a breath that sent her bangs flying upward as she walked toward him. She looked so damn sexy, he wanted to feather his fingers through the strands.

Good grief. How long had it been since he’d been laid?

He couldn’t remember. He’d been so damned focused on working and saving money for his own spread that his personal life had been put on the back burner. That was the only reason he was attracted to this uppity lawyer lady.

Only she didn’t seem quite as uppity as he’d first thought. With her hair tangled around her cheeks, she looked downright earthy. He wondered what she’d look like if she ever let go.

She paused at the door, her gaze dark and intense. “I found pictures of Sondra inside. Thacker definitely had an unhealthy obsession with her.”

Cash clenched his jaw. “You find anything else?”

She shook her head. “No signs of Tyler or that he’d been in the house.”

“You know if he was watching Sondra, even if he didn’t kill her, he could have seen the person who did.”

“I’ll ask him.’ BJ said.

“Check the pictures. Maybe he caught someone else watching her in one of the pictures he took.”

“Good point.” BJ examined each one, scrutinizing the backgrounds. “I don’t see anything here.”

Cash sucked in a breath. “I searched the exterior. No root cellar or emergency fallout shelter where he could have hidden Tyler.”

BJ reached for the wooden door to the barn. “Then let’s look in here.” She jiggled the latch, but it was locked. Cash scanned the area, then spotted some tools in a corner of the makeshift carport. He found a pair of bolt cutters, then broke the lock.

Cash held his breath and paused to listen as she opened the door.

BJ PULLED A small flashlight from her pocket and waved it around the interior of the barn. With the two windows boarded up, the space was dark, and a stench permeated the air.

A low sound, like scratching, drifted to her, and she paused. Tyler? Was he locked inside something in here?

She scanned the floor and walls. Shelves had been built on the far side, and farm tools hung nearby. A wooden door to the left probably led to a tack room. She crossed to it, then jiggled the knob, but the door wouldn't open.

It had been nailed shut.

"Something's inside." Cash grabbed a tool from the wall, rushed back to her and used the tool to rip out the nails. Wood cracked and splintered. Cash jerked the door open and BJ shone the flashlight across the space. Dirt and straw on the floor. An old saddle and ratty blanket on the wall.

"I don't see anything," BJ murmured.

Cash gestured toward the corner. The wood in

the corner was rotting, and several boards were cracked. He yanked one away. "Looks like raccoons got in."

BJ covered her nose as the stench grew heavier.

"Two dead inside the wall," Cash pointed out. Animal droppings. "Looks like there might have been a whole family, but the others got out."

Relieved it wasn't Tyler, BJ sighed and backed from the room. Cash followed, his own relief palpable in the breath he exhaled.

"There's nothing here," BJ said.

Cash lifted the flashlight and aimed it toward the back of the barn. "There's another door."

BJ followed him past the tools, weaving between a rusted wheelbarrow and a bundle of hay. Cash pushed the door open, and they stepped into a pen that led to two stalls.

Hay bales were stacked in one corner. Cash headed toward them. Was Tyler behind the bales?

Cash lifted one and threw it to the side, and BJ jumped in to help. One by one, they moved the bales until they could see behind the stack.

Nothing.

Relief blended with disappointment. Where was Tyler? Was he on this ranch or were they wasting precious time?

THE BARN WAS EMPTY.

If Tyler was on the ranch, where was he?

Cash's gut tightened. What if the boy was here but he wasn't alive? There were acres of land where Thacker could have hidden—or buried—him.

Nausea rose to his throat. Surely to God Thacker wouldn't have been so cruel.

Cash stepped outside into the pen and searched the ground for freshly turned earth. The soil was dry, flat, with hay scattered around as if the wind had blown it into the pen.

He opened the gate and scanned the area, then noticed footprints in the dirt. Following the path the footprints made, he walked up the hill, where they ended by a cottonwood.

He sucked in a breath. The grass beneath the tree was patchy, the dirt disturbed. It also created a small mound.

Fear shot through him. The mound was small—the perfect size for a child's grave.

# *Chapter Thirteen*

BJ sensed something was wrong.

Cash had rushed up the hill as if he'd found something. Now he stood ramrod straight, his head bowed, his face strained.

She took a deep breath and hurried to join him, her heels digging into the dirt. When she reached the cottonwood, she gently touched his shoulder. "Cash, what is it?"

He pivoted, the grim expression in his eyes tearing at her heart. Then he gestured toward the ground.

BJ's chest clenched at the sight of the mound of dirt. Denial screamed in her head as the memory of her own son's grave flashed before her. Her pulse quickened. A dizzy spell overcame her, and she staggered sideways.

"I'm going to get a shovel," Cash said gruffly.

A fine sheen of perspiration coated BJ's neck, and she leaned against the tree and forced calming breaths just as her therapist had taught her. For months after she'd lost her husband and son, she hadn't wanted to go on. She'd wanted to join the two of them in heaven.

Her therapist assured her those feelings were normal, that she just needed time to heal. Everyone told her the grief would lessen over time.

It hadn't. Sometimes a picture or a song or seeing another child brought it all back, pain so raw that she felt as if she was drowning in it.

The wind kicked up, shaking the leaves and adding a chill to her already trembling body. Her vision blurred.

Her little boy's face appeared. *It's okay, Mommy. I love you.*

Tears burned her eyes, and she blinked, willing them not to fall until she was back at the cabin, alone.

One slipped down her cheek, anyway.

Reality returned as Cash appeared with a shovel. His hand brushed her cheek. "BJ?"

She sighed, stifling emotions that had a will of their own.

"Are you okay?" Cash asked, his voice low. Concerned.

She brushed the tear away. "He can't be in there, Cash. He just can't."

His mouth tightened, then he gave her arm a quick, soft squeeze. "Go back to the car. I'll let you know when I finish."

She shook her head. She had to be here. If Tyler was in the ground and Cash dug him up, the police would have dozens of questions. Why was Cash at the grave? How did he know where the boy's body was?

Because he'd buried him…

CASH CLENCHED THE shovel with a white-knuckled grip. BJ looked as if she was going to faint. Was she just worried about Tyler, or was something else wrong?

He touched her hand and her skin felt clammy. "At least sit down, BJ. You don't look well."

She nodded weakly, then stumbled a few feet away from the mound, sank onto the grass and leaned her head back against the tree. "You should wait on Deputy Whitefeather."

"If he's searching the farm, he may be a while." And Cash had to know if Tyler was buried here. He sensed BJ did, too.

"We still need to wait, Cash. If there's a body and you contaminate it with your prints, it'll be hard to prove that you didn't put it there."

Cash jammed the shovel into the ground. Anger, worry for Tyler and anxiety fueled his adrenaline, and he paced back and forth. "You can't think I'd put a little boy in the ground."

BJ shook her head. "I don't, but believing you and proving your innocence are two different things. If I'm going to clear you, you have to take my advice."

"Of course I want you to clear me, but Tyler is more important." Although if Tyler was buried by the tree, it was too late to save him.

That fear made his knees give way. He caught himself and stiffened his spine. Dead or alive, he'd find Tyler, and he'd make whoever took him pay.

An engine rumbled, and Deputy Whitefeather's SUV chugged down the graveled drive. Hope spiked that Whitefeather had found Tyler safe. Cash rushed down the hill toward the SUV.

Whitefeather slid from the driver's side and Thacker from the passenger seat. Cash gave the deputy a questioning look.

"No sign of Tyler," Deputy Whitefeather said in a low voice.

"I told you, I didn't take the boy," Thacker said. "You're wasting time talking to me when you should be looking for him."

Cash cleared his throat. "There's a grave at the top of the hill, Thacker."

Whitefeather pivoted, leveling Thacker with a suspicious look. "You buried someone on your property?"

Thacker bounced his leg up and down. "No, it's my dog. He died a couple of months ago."

Whitefeather crooked his head toward the hill. "Let's see."

"You've got to be kidding," Thacker said in a childish whine.

"Kidnapping and murder are not anything to joke about," Whitefeather said.

"I…didn't mean it like that," Thacker argued.

"I found a shovel." Cash pointed to BJ. "We were waiting on you." BJ *had* insisted, but the deputy didn't have to know that.

Whitefeather jerked his thumb at Thacker. "Come on, let's see if you're telling the truth."

Thacker glared at Cash, but led the way. Cash followed behind Whitefeather, his pulse hammering.

If Thacker was lying and they found Tyler in that grave, he'd kill the son of a bitch with his bare hands.

BJ STRUGGLED TO pull herself together. For a year after her son's death, she'd dropped out of work and life. Slowly, she'd made a comeback, and then taken the job at her father's firm.

Although they disagreed ethically about certain cases, she'd needed a safe place to heal.

But the missing little boy resurrected the grief she'd struggled to bury.

Cash's love for the child was obvious, too. The terror in his eyes when he'd shown her that grave reeked of pain and fear. The kind of fear a parent felt for a child.

Deputy Whitefeather approached with Thacker and Cash. His brows furrowed as he glanced at her. "You okay?"

She nodded.

"The kid's not in there," Thacker said. "My bloodhound Clyde is."

BJ twisted her hands together but said nothing. Cash walked over and stood beside her, his hands jammed in his pockets as the deputy began to dig.

Gray clouds moved across the sky, shrouding the sun and casting a gloominess to the land. The wind shook the trees again, sending a shiver through BJ. The sound of the shovel hitting dirt and rock echoed in the quiet.

Thacker shifted on the balls of his feet, his

breath rattling. The deputy dug deeper, slinging dirt and gravel and grass to the side of the mound.

A half foot down, the shovel hit something hard. Cash peered into the hole, a low sound erupting in his throat.

"Bones."

BJ's lungs squeezed for air.

"I told you, my dog is buried there," Thacker said, his voice warbling.

Deputy Whitefeather knelt and raked dirt away with his hands, gently scooping more out. BJ watched him carefully working away at the grave so as not to disturb the remains.

Tense seconds passed. The sun slipped away for the night. The air turned chilly, a gust of wind picking up twigs and scattering them about. Somewhere an animal howled, and a dog barked.

Whitefeather shone a light into the hole, then raked another section of dirt from the bones. He murmured something in his native dialect, then gestured toward the lower part of the skeleton.

"It is a dog," he said, relief in his voice.

"How can you be sure?" Cash asked.

"I worked with a vet on the reservation." Deputy Whitefeather pointed to a section of remains. "There are four canine femurs. This jaw structure supports Thacker's statement about his bloodhound."

Relief flooded BJ. If Tyler wasn't buried here, there was a chance he was still alive.

CASH RELEASED THE breath he'd been holding. Thank God Tyler wasn't in the ground.

Knowing that meant that they might still be able to save him. If they could find out where the hell he was and who'd taken him.

"I told you," Thacker snarled.

Cash started toward him, but Whitefeather laid a hand on his back. "It's not worth it, Cash. Let's go."

The deputy was big and tall, but Cash rivaled him in size. Still, his gruff, quiet control forced Cash to reach for his own and reel in his temper. He didn't want to go back to jail.

He wanted to find that little boy.

BJ stood, regaining her composure. "Mr. Thacker, you've been watching Sondra. Maybe you saw something that could help us. Was anyone else following her?"

Thacker shook his head. "Not that I saw."

Judging from the pictures, he'd been too focused on Sondra to have noticed anything else.

The deputy handed the shovel to Thacker so he could cover the dog's skeleton with dirt. "Mr. Thacker, we may need to talk to you again. Don't leave town."

Thacker spewed curse words, but Whitefeather held his head high as he strode toward the SUV. Cash couldn't shake the feeling that something was seriously wrong with BJ as they followed the deputy.

He would find out. But he wouldn't press her in front of the deputy.

"Where to now?" BJ asked Whitefeather.

"I'm going to talk to Sondra's girlfriend. Diane Stuckey."

"We'll follow you. I'd like to speak to her, too," BJ said. "Cash can wait in the truck."

"Like he did at Thacker's," Whitefeather said wryly.

"I didn't interfere," Cash said.

"You pointed out that grave. If Tyler had been buried there, the DA would have argued that you led us to his body because you put him in the ground."

"That's ridiculous," Cash muttered.

"He's right," BJ said.

Cash clenched his hands into fists. "I swear I won't interfere. But I need to hear what Diane has to say."

He just hoped to hell she knew something helpful.

BJ STUDIED THE condominium complex where Diane Stuckey lived. It was a new development on the outskirts of Pistol Whip that catered to the thirtysomething crowd. Residents enjoyed views of the countryside, but also had the amenities of a big city development.

Deputy Whitefeather identified himself to security at the gate, parked, then slid from the SUV. BJ parked behind him.

Each condo had its own single-car garage, yet several expensive cars were parked in the driveways.

"Koker, you've met this lady before?" Deputy Whitefeather asked Cash as they headed up the sidewalk.

Cash nodded. "She visited Sondra when I worked at the Wagon Wheel. They met in high school and were best friends. I think they showed horses together."

"Is she married?" BJ asked.

"Not that I know of, but I didn't talk to Sondra very much the past few months. I took all the work I could get." He rubbed the back of his neck. "Besides, Elmore didn't want me on his land, so I didn't push it."

Whitefeather gestured toward Diane's unit, a light gray, two-story stucco that faced the east, offering beautiful views of the sunrise. Colorful wind chimes dangled from a horse figure carved out of metal.

The deputy punched the doorbell, which delivered a musical sound. Seconds later, the door opened and a striking brunette dressed in a designer suit and stilettos greeted them. "Hello."

Deputy Whitefeather introduced himself and BJ, then Cash threw up a hand. "Hey, Diane."

She folded her arms across her chest, making her ample bosom protrude even more. "I can't believe you'd show up here, Cash. I thought you were in jail."

"He's out on bail," BJ said. "I'm representing Mr. Koker. We need to ask you some questions."

"I've already talked to Sheriff Jasper."

"It'll just take a moment," BJ said quietly.

A wary look settled on Diane's face, but she invited them inside. The woman's condo reminded BJ of her father's house—everything was decorator perfect. White furniture, expensive vases, artwork that should have been in a museum, not a home. The place felt cold and empty.

She'd thought Diane and Sondra were best friends, but judging from their lifestyles and the photos she'd seen of Sondra and Tyler, Sondra was definitely more down to earth.

Diane escorted them to the living room and offered sparkling water, tea or coffee, but they declined. She poured herself a glass of mineral water, then sank into a plush white chair. "Deputy Whitefeather, Mr. Elmore called me when he first heard about Sondra. I…can't believe she's gone." The woman shot an accusatory look toward Cash. "She and I have been friends since grade school. We competed in dressage competitions together, were both cheerleaders and in the homecoming court. Then we roomed together our first year in college."

"You must be devastated over losing her," BJ said, although the woman didn't look devastated. She looked as if she was about to go out on the town.

Diane plucked a tissue from the end table and dabbed at her eyes. "I am. I…can't believe she's gone. That someone murdered her."

"I didn't kill her," Cash said gruffly. "Do you have any idea who did, Diane?"

She sniffed and shook her head.

"Was she dating anyone?" BJ asked.

Diane wadded the tissue in her hand. "Not that I know of. But after Tyler was born, she dropped out of the dating scene. Although she did mention that some guy was bothering her."

"Ronnie Thacker?" BJ asked.

She nodded.

"We've already spoken to him," the deputy said.

"Excuse me, Diane," Cash said. "Could I use your restroom?"

Diane frowned, but gave a slight nod. "It's down the hall on the left."

"Thanks."

BJ glanced at Cash, but he gave nothing away. What was he up to?

He slipped into the hallway.

"Do you really think he's innocent?" Diane asked.

"I do," BJ said. "Why? Do you have reason to believe Cash was dangerous?"

Diane shrugged, then picked at a piece of invisible lint on her suit jacket. "I guess not. I always thought he was in love with Sondra, but she said they were only friends."

"Do you know who fathered Tyler?" Deputy Whitefeather asked bluntly.

Diane shook her head. "She told everyone it was Cash, but she told me she hadn't slept with Cash. She swore me to secrecy though."

"So she didn't tell you his name?"

"No. She said no one needed to know."

"Do you think she was afraid of Tyler's father?" the deputy asked.

Diane's eyes widened. "You think Tyler's father killed Sondra and took Tyler?"

"I don't know," BJ said. "But Cash is innocent, so that means that Sondra's killer is still out there, and Tyler may be in danger now."

Diane looked down at her manicured nails. "I'm sure Tyler is fine."

"Why do you say that?" Deputy Whitefeather asked.

Panic flashed in Diane's eyes. "I…just hope he is, that's all. I mean, why would anyone hurt him?"

"Maybe he saw the person who killed his mother," BJ suggested.

Panic flared again, and Diane walked over to the window.

BJ wanted to push her more, but the deputy's cell phone trilled. He removed it from his pocket and connected the call. "Yeah? Okay, I'll be right there."

When he disconnected, he stood abruptly. "I need to go, Miss Alexander."

Footsteps echoed in the hallway and Cash appeared. "What's going on?" he asked.

Deputy Whitefeather clenched his jaw. "That was Maddox. Elmore just received a ransom call."

# *Chapter Fourteen*

Cash's heart raced. A ransom demand was a good sign.

Deputy Whitefeather turned to Diane. "Thank you for your time, Miss Stuckey. If you think of someone who had a grudge against Sondra or her father, or anything she said about the baby's father, give me a call." He placed a business card in her hand. "Sometimes even the smallest detail can break a case."

Diane studied the number for a moment, then laid the card on the side table. "I will." She bit her lower lip. "I…hope you find Tyler and that he's all right. Sondra…loved that little boy more than her own life."

Cash agreed. Had she died trying to protect him from something? Or somebody?

BJ left her card on the table beside the deputy's. "Cash, let's go." She brushed his arm with her fingertips, and Cash followed her and the deputy outside.

"What were the ransom demands?" Cash asked.

"A million," Deputy Whitefeather replied. "Kidnapper said he'd call back later with instructions."

"Did they trace the call?" BJ asked.

The deputy shook his head. "Call was too short to trace and the voice sounded altered. Probably used a computer. The lab is going to see if they can work their magic."

They separated to go to their vehicles. Just as they were leaving, Diane rushed out and jumped in her BMW.

"Did you find anything in Diane's house?" BJ asked.

Cash tensed. "What do you mean? I just went to the—"

"Come on, Cash," BJ said. "We all know that

was an excuse for you to look around. Did you see anything suspicious?"

He grunted a no. "There's no sign that Tyler has been at Diane's house. No kids' clothes. No toys. Every room is immaculate. Like a damn glass house."

"Hmm. Sondra's place was homey. Makes me wonder if Sondra and Diane were really that close lately." BJ looked pensive. "Sondra seemed like a loving mother, like she'd settled down, and Diane is still into the party scene."

Cash's heart squeezed. "True." If Sondra hadn't been too young for him, and Elmore's daughter, he might have fallen for her.

But he hadn't.

He *had* admired the way she loved her son, though. Every little boy needed a devoted mother like her. Cash sure as hell hadn't had one.

His breath caught. Or had he?

If he was a McCullen, his mother and father had wanted him. What if whoever had taken Tyler dumped him with strangers or on some church doorstep? What if whoever found him didn't report it?

No telling where the kid might be now.

BJ'S PHONE BUZZED with a text. From Diane.

Remembered the name of a rancher Elmore drove into bankruptcy. Sondra said she was afraid of him. His name is Dale Nix.

"I'm going to do rounds in town, then head to Elmore's," Deputy Whitefeather said. "I'll see you guys back at the ranch."

"We'll meet you at Elmore's," Cash said.

"No," Whitefeather said. "Maddox said he'd call you when he knew something."

Frustration creased Cash's face. BJ wanted to go to Elmore's, too, but she trusted Maddox.

"He's right, Cash," BJ said. "Maddox is on our side."

Cash looked grim-faced, but gave a quick nod. The deputy started the engine and drove away from the condominium complex. Night had set in, gloomy shadows darkening the landscape as he pulled onto the highway.

BJ gently touched his hand. “Cash, Diane texted me with the name of a man Elmore drove into bankruptcy.”

Cash sucked in a breath. “He could be after money to get back at Elmore.”

BJ nodded. “Let’s go see him.”

“BJ, someone almost killed us earlier. I think you should stay out of it and let me handle it.”

Fear gnawed at BJ as an image of her car going over that ridge flashed behind her eyes. She had been terrified.

But a little boy’s life was at stake and she refused to let the kidnapper intimidate her. “I appreciate your concern, Cash, but I’m not giving into a threat. Tyler needs us.”

Cash’s gaze met hers, tension seeping between them.

“Just tell me where to go,” Cash said.

BJ used her phone to research Nix. “Nix lives in public housing about thirty miles from Pistol Whip. His wife had a heart attack and died a month after they lost the ranch."

"If he blames Elmore for his bankruptcy, he may also blame him for his wife's death."

"That would be motive," BJ agreed.

BJ gave him directions to the housing development where Nix had moved. Storm clouds rolled in, the wind kicking up and stirring dust and blowing it across the highway as the truck chugged toward town.

The rumbling of the engine echoed through the cab. BJ's silence stood between them, a bridge he didn't know how to cross. He wanted to ask about her personal life. Why the grave at the tree had upset her so much.

He would find out.

But first they had to talk to Nix. He could have killed Sondra. He could have Tyler.

They had to hurry.

# *Chapter Fifteen*

BJ winced as night shadows plagued the roads. She couldn't imagine the terror little Tyler was feeling. He needed to be home in his own bed with his mama reading him a story and tucking him in.

That would never happen again. Just as she would never tuck her own son into his bed.

Grief threatened to overwhelm her, but she tamped it back.

Cash parked in front of the low-income housing development, and they climbed out. Knowing Nix had moved from a hundred-acre spread to this tiny, tired-looking concrete block building roused her sympathy. On top of that, he'd lost his wife.

The units were connected, the only grassy area a small shared space in front of the building. No kids' toys or bikes. A black, beat-up pickup was parked in front of Nix's unit.

Cash strode to the door and knocked.

"Let me handle this, Cash," BJ said.

He shot her an irritated look. She understood his frustration, but she didn't want to see him locked up again. "Please, Cash. I'm not trying to clip your wings—I'm trying to keep you out of jail. Help me do my job."

He nodded solemnly.

Footsteps echoed from the other side. A short, chubby man with a gray beard and wire-rimmed glasses answered the door. He reeked of whiskey.

BJ introduced herself and Cash, earning a deep-set frown from Nix. "What the hell do you want?" he asked.

"We need to talk to you about Lester Elmore," BJ said. "You accused him of driving you into bankruptcy."

Nix scratched his beard. "You here to help me get my farm back?"

BJ bit the inside of her cheek. She hated deceiving the man, but Tyler's life depended on them finding the truth. "We'll see if you have a case. Right now we need you to tell us about Elmore. When did you last see or talk to him?"

"Been months," Nix said. "The day the bank foreclosed on me. He and the damn banker were buddies. Both damn vultures. Elmore was just waiting the days out. Picked up my place for next to nothing."

"That must have made you angry," BJ said.

"Damn right it did," Nix said. "Wife was devastated over losing our house. We lived there for forty years. Raised our boys on that land."

BJ's heart squeezed. "I'm sorry. I'm sure that was difficult."

"Broke her spirit. She had a heart attack the week we moved."

"You hated Elmore, didn't you?" Cash cut in. "You blamed him for her death."

Nix narrowed his eyes at Cash. "Sure did. Elmore refused me water rights, made it impossible for me to keep up my land and herd. That's why I couldn't pay the bills."

"Did you know his daughter, Sondra?" BJ asked.

Nix scowled. "I knew he had one, but I never met her. Heard in town he was mighty protective of her."

"He was," Cash said.

Suspicion flared in Nix's eyes. "What is this really about?"

BJ debated on how to approach him, then decided to be direct. "Mr. Elmore's daughter, Sondra, was murdered."

Nix pulled a hand down his chin. "I heard about that. That was too bad."

"Whoever killed her kidnapped her son, Tyler," Cash said bluntly.

Nix's eyes widened in alarm, then with the realization that he was a suspect.

"I hated Elmore," the man said. "But ain't no way I'd kill a woman or kidnap no kid." He jerked his thumb toward the parking lot. "Now leave, and don't come back."

A second later, he slammed the door in their faces.

BJ's phone buzzed with a text.

Ransom drop tonight. Midnight. Stone Gap.

She angled the phone so Cash could read the text.

"I want to be there," Cash said.

BJ shook her head. "Cash, let Maddox handle this."

A muscle jumped in his cheek. "If the kidnapper brings Tyler, he'll be scared. He needs a friendly face."

He was right. But convincing Maddox would be a challenge. She punched in his number.

"What exactly did the kidnapper say? Is he bringing Tyler to the drop site?" she asked.

"He didn't give details," Maddox said. "Instructions were for Elmore to come alone."

"Could be a setup," BJ said. "He takes the money and kills Elmore."

"I know."

Cash grabbed the phone from her. "If you think this is a setup, let me go as Elmore," Cash said. "I'll wear his hat and clothes and make the drop."

BJ clenched his arm. "That's too dangerous, Cash."

"I don't give a damn. All that matters is saving Tyler."

CASH MET MADDOX at Elmore's door, braced for an argument.

Maddox led him and BJ into the study, where Elmore was pacing, his cell phone gripped in his hand. "I don't give a damn if I'm penalized by pulling money from that account," he bellowed. "I need cash and I need it tonight."

Sheriff Jasper was standing close by, his arms folded. He looked up at Maddox and Cash with a scowl. "What are you doing here?" Jasper bellowed.

"Working a kidnapping case," Maddox said bluntly.

Jasper cursed. "I can handle it."

"No way," Maddox said. "This is my jurisdiction."

Rage flared in Jasper's eyes, rage directed toward Cash. "And what are you doing here?"

Cash cleared his throat as Elmore hung up and faced them. "Trying to find a missing little boy."

"Or trying to make sure Elmore pays," Jasper said.

Cash barely held back from slugging the bastard. "I want to deliver the ransom," Cash said. "I'll do whatever it takes to bring Tyler home safely."

Elmore hung up the phone, his nostrils flaring. "Maybe you're offering 'cause you set this whole thing up and you know who has my grandson."

Cash whirled on him. "That's ridiculous, Elmore. You know I cared about Tyler. I spent a hell of a lot more time with him than you did."

Elmore went ashen-faced. "Is that why you did this? So you could be the hero? You thought if you saved him, I'd let you see him whenever you wanted."

Cash balled his hands into fists. "I would

never have hurt Sondra or scared Tyler. We were friends." Fear clogged his throat. "If you let me help you get him back, I'll walk away and you'll never see me again."

An undercurrent of anxiety and distrust charged the air as Elmore studied him.

Maddox cleared his throat. "Cash didn't take the boy or kill your daughter."

"He's been with me ever since he was released from jail," BJ stated, backing up Maddox.

"Let me do this for you," Cash said. "If it's a trap, you could get hurt, Mr. Elmore. Then Tyler would have lost all his family. He's going to need you when he comes home and learns his mother's gone. If he doesn't already know."

Jasper put his hand on Elmore's shoulder. "Don't listen to him."

Elmore scrubbed a shaky hand over his face, then sank onto the leather sofa in the seating area. "What if the kidnapper recognizes it's not me?"

"I'll wear your clothes, your hat, your glasses," Cash said.

"No, Cash, I'll do it," Maddox said.

Cash shook his head. “That won’t work, Maddox. You’re too tall. I’m more Elmore’s height.”

Maddox seemed to stew over that for a second.

“Besides, you need to be there to make the arrest,” Cash pointed out.

Maddox sighed heavily. He couldn’t argue with that.

Cash’s pulse jumped. “Now, let’s make a plan.”

Maddox shifted and crossed his arms again. “The instructions said to leave the duffel bag of money at Stone Gap. When they confirm it’s there, the kidnapper will send Tyler to you,” Maddox said. “That means he’ll probably be watching from a distance. He won’t be close enough to tell that it’s Cash instead of you.”

“I don’t think this is a good idea,” Jasper said.

Elmore threw up a warning hand. “Stay out of it, Jasper. Right now I just want Tyler back.”

Jasper muttered an oath, shot Cash and Maddox and BJ a dark look, then stormed out the door.

Elmore pressed his knuckles to his eyes and rubbed them. He looked weak. Frail. Broken.

Nothing like the astute arrogant bastard who’d

fired Cash and pressured his daughter to give away her child.

"You'll bring the boy back to me," Elmore said.

Cash nodded. "Yes, sir." He'd bring him back or die trying.

BJ DIDN'T LIKE the situation. Although, if Elmore paid the ransom, hopefully they'd get his grandson back. They might even get lucky and catch the kidnapper.

Elmore's phone buzzed again. He glanced at the number. "My accountant. I have to take this. He's working on securing the ransom money."

He stepped over to his desk, and BJ motioned to Maddox that she wanted to talk. Cash joined them in the hallway. "Did you check out Elmore's financials?" she murmured.

"Of course I did, but he appears clean," Maddox said. "Why? Do you have information?"

BJ tucked a strand of hair behind one ear. "No. He seems truly upset and worried about the little boy. But he might have taken out an insurance policy on Sondra and Tyler. If he was in financial trouble, he could have agreed to a kidnapping. But things went south. Sondra might have been killed trying to keep that kidnapping from happening."

"No kidnapping insurance on the child," Maddox said. "He did have a life insurance policy on Sondra, but Tyler was the recipient."

BJ arched a brow. "And if Tyler's gone?"

"Money goes to Elmore," Maddox said.

Cash made a low sound in his throat. "If that man killed his own daughter and put Tyler through this, he's a monster."

"If he did, he'll pay," Maddox said. "But we have to go by the book. Elmore agreed to having his phones tapped so we can monitor all communication between him and anyone else. So far, there's nothing to indicate that Elmore set this up."

"He'd better not have," Cash muttered.

Maddox adjusted his Stetson, worry creasing his face. "You're going to make the drop, Cash, but I'll be close by, watching your back. Whitefeather is staying with Elmore, and Brett agreed to keep an eye on Nix."

Elmore appeared in the doorway, wiping sweat from his forehead with a monogrammed handkerchief. "My accountant got the cash. He'll be here in half an hour."

"Let's go over the plan," Maddox said. "Mr. Elmore, please get some of your clothes, one of your hats, something recognizable so we can pull this switch off."

Elmore gave Cash a sharp look, but removed his signet ring. "This was specially made for me by the Cattleman's Club in honor of my achievements and leadership. I never go anywhere without it."

Cash's jaw snapped tight as he accepted the ring. It was snug but he managed to get it on. "I'll bring it back, sir."

"Don't worry about the ring. Just bring my grandson home."

BJ bit her lower lip. She had to consider Elmore as a suspect, but the fear and anguish in his voice sounded real.

Cash's eyes darkened with worry, too.

Her heart stuttered. God, he was just the kind

of man she admired. He loved the land, the outdoors, and even though he'd never had a break in his life, he still fought for what was right.

Admiration for him stirred along with concern. What if this meet was a setup and he got hurt?

Fear seized her. She'd vowed not to care about another man. Not to fall for Cash's sexy, bad-boy looks.

But how could she not fall for Cash? He was the sexiest and bravest man she'd ever met.

He'd risked his life to save hers. She couldn't ignore the importance of that.

And he was willing to give up his life for this child, a child who wasn't even his son.

THE EVENING DRAGGED by as they finalized the plans for the drop. Elmore's accountant showed up with the money, marked bills tucked between unmarked ones, to enable them to eventually trace the kidnapper—if he escaped.

Elmore shocked Cash by venturing into the guesthouse and retrieving pictures of Tyler—a scrapbook of memories Sondra had put together. Elmore's hand shook as he flipped the pages.

It seemed the fear of losing Tyler was sinking in, and he was probably regretting not being part of the boy's life while he had the chance.

Cash disappeared into one of the guest rooms and dressed in Elmore's clothing: a pair of expensive jeans that Cash wouldn't be caught dead in and a custom-tailored Western shirt that bore a symbol for the ranch. Both fit snugly, especially with the bullet proof vest Maddox insisted he wear, but he could make it work.

Maddox attached a wire to Cash's chest before he buttoned the shirt, then gave him a tiny earphone so Maddox could communicate with him.

Elmore's Stetson and a pair of sunglasses helped camouflage his face. Elmore's boots, slightly too tight, were trimmed with gold spurs that sparkled, and probably cost a small fortune.

Cash and Maddox descended the steps and joined BJ, Elmore and Whitefeather in the study. BJ fidgeted, her expression anxious, but Whitefeather gave him a small smile of approval as if he thought the disguise might work.

Elmore lifted a tumbler of Scotch and took a sip, his eyes assessing. “Square your shoulders and act like you’re somebody,” he grunted.

Cash glared at the man, but stiffened and stood more erect.

“The money’s in that bag,” Elmore said. “Go get my grandson.”

“I will.” Cash grabbed the keys to his truck, but Elmore shook his head. Then he pulled a set of keys from his pocket. “Show up in that piece of junk and whoever has Tyler will know it’s not me.” He shoved the keys at Cash. “Take mine.”

Cash sucked in a breath. Elmore’s Cadillac was pricey. What if he wrecked the damn thing?

BJ approached, her eyes dark with concern. “Maddox and I are going with you.”

Cash shook his head. “The instructions said for Elmore to come alone. If the kidnapper’s watching, he’ll see you.”

“I’ll be hunched in the backseat,” BJ said.

"No way," Cash said. "I won't put you in danger."

"He's right," Maddox said to BJ. "I'll park a safe distance away in some bushes, then hike in on foot and cover you, Cash."

Nervous tension knotted Cash's stomach. Tyler's life might lie in his hands. What if he messed this up?

BJ squeezed his arm. "You can do this, Cash. Tyler needs you."

Cash swallowed hard. Her faith in him made his chest ache. No one had ever believed in him before.

Maddox checked his watch. "It's time. Are you ready, Cash?"

Cash nodded. "Let's do it."

Elmore started to follow them outside, but Maddox pressed a hand to his chest. "Stay inside until you hear from me. If this perp is watching your house, we don't want him to see that we made a switch."

Elmore hesitated but agreed. "Just don't let Tyler get hurt."

Maddox offered a tentative smile. "We'll do our best."

Cash and Maddox stepped aside for a moment to check the mike before he got into the car.

"Don't try to be a hero, Cash," Maddox said. "Just park, get out and drop the money where the kidnapper instructed you to, then sit tight in the car. Hopefully, the kidnapper will send Tyler in on foot. If not, he should send us word where to find him."

"I understand."

Cash started the engine, eased from Elmore's drive, then followed the GPS directions to the drop spot. As he maneuvered the rocky road to Stone Gap, a desolate stretch of Wyoming with a natural ravine and giant boulders and trails that led through the scrub, a dozen possible scenarios traipsed through his mind.

So many things could go wrong.

No. Nothing could go wrong.

Cash steered the Cadillac around a curve, then passed the sign for Stone Gap and drove along the graveled road to the drop-off spot. He scanned the area in search of a car or someone hovering in the bushes.

Someone who planned to kill Elmore, take his money and run.

A noise jarred him. Was someone out there? Maybe they were coming up behind him?

He glanced in the rearview mirror, then cursed. Dammit, BJ had stowed away in the back floor.

"What are you doing?" he barked. "I told you to stay at Elmore's."

BJ released a breath. "I wanted to be with you in case you get Tyler."

"It's too dangerous, BJ." He checked his watch. Dammit. He didn't have time to take her back to Elmore's.

"I'll stay in the car," BJ whispered. "But if Tyler's scared and upset, I can help."

That was true. But he didn't like it one bit.

And now he had to worry about keeping BJ safe.

Sweat beaded on his lower lip as he parked. The sky was gloomy, the wind picking up, stirring dust and sending tumbleweed across the desolate terrain. An animal's howl echoed from the deep cluster of bushes on the hill. He narrowed his eyes, scrutinizing the trees and rocks.

"What's going on?" Maddox said into his ear piece.

Cash gritted his teeth. "BJ stowed away in the back seat."

A litany of profanity spewed from Maddox. "That was stupid."

Cash bit back a comment of agreement. "She thinks she can help if we get Tyler and he's frightened."

"Tell her to stay in the damn car," Maddox said. "This kidnapper is not playing games."

"I know that," BJ snapped from the back seat.

"I'll make sure she stays put," Cash said.

Maddox heaved a sigh of frustration. "All right, it's too late to turn back now. We might create suspicion. Go ahead and make the drop."

Cash tugged the hat low on his head to shadow his face, grabbed the bag, opened the car door and slowly climbed out. Elmore's ring felt heavy on his hand as he gripped the duffel bag.

With every breath he took, he visually searched for an ambush.

The animal howled again—a mountain lion?

He went still, afraid to move too quickly in case it was waiting to attack. Seconds passed. The bushes parted and a streak of orange flashed past, quickly gliding from one rock to another.

Pulse pounding, he slowly inched up the small hill to the rock formation.

Elmore's boots dug into the dirt, the wind swirling dust at his feet as he lowered the bag to the ground. Just as he descended the small hill, a shot rang out.

The bullet skimmed past his head, then another one sailed at him. He ducked to avoid it, his gaze scanning the bushes.

The bullet zinged by his head and nearly clipped him.

# *Chapter Sixteen*

Cash braced his gun at the ready, then peered above the rocks where he'd hidden, searching for the shooter.

The shots had come from his left. Higher. On the hill, he spotted a giant boulder where the shooter could be hiding.

He fired his weapon toward it. A bullet pinged off the rock and hit the ground.

He watched, waiting on the shooter to move or fire back.

Instead, tree branches swayed above. The bastard was getting away!

He swung a glance at the duffel bag. It was gone.

"Cash?" Maddox bellowed in his ear. "Are you hit, man?"

"No, I'm good," he said, as he continued to peruse the area. "Where is the son of a bitch?"

"Headed toward the top of the ridge. Must have a car there."

"The money's gone."

"I know. There are two of them. I saw a figure in black snatch it and run." Maddox's breath heaved out. "I'm going after the shooter."

A dark figure caught Cash's eye. To his left. On a path that led to a scenic overhang.

"I'll follow the money." Cash kept his eyes trained on the figure as he darted down the hill and jogged toward the Cadillac.

BJ was running toward him. "Cash!"

"I told you to stay in the car," he growled.

She caught his arm. "Are you hurt?"

"No." He ushered her back to the car, ignoring the fear in her eyes. "Now get in," he rasped. "We need to go."

BJ slid into the seat, and he jogged around the front of the car and jumped in. A quick flick of the switch and the car sputtered to life.

He threw the car into Drive, swung it around

and raced over the graveled road to a parking area. Just as they reached it, a dark green SUV tore from the lot.

Cash stomped on the gas and sped after it. The SUV's tires screeched as it roared down the incline. The Cadillac's tires churned over gravel as he followed.

"Did you see the shooter?" BJ asked.

"No, he was up higher." He swung a right, desperate to keep up with the SUV as they careened around a curve. "Did you see anything?"

"No." She gripped the dash as he made the turn on two wheels.

"Is Tyler in the car?"

BJ leaned forward, eyes narrowing as she searched. "I can't see anything. The windows are tinted."

Cash cursed. "Tyler had better be in there."

"You said there were two," BJ's voice cracked. "The shooter might have him."

Cash swallowed hard to control his panic. The fact that they had been ambushed was a bad sign.

Tyler might not be with either one of them. He

might be dead, just like Sondra, and this was a setup to extract enough money for the kidnappers to escape.

TERROR SHOT THROUGH BJ.

If Tyler wasn't in the car, the kidnappers could have left him somewhere safe. Maybe they'd planned to get the money, then go back, pick up Tyler, drop him somewhere, then call Elmore and tell him where he was.

Or they might not have planned to give him back at all.

Cash hit a pothole and the vehicle bounced, jarring her even more. She clawed at the seat to keep upright as he swung to the left and sped up on the SUV. Seconds turned into minutes as he chased it onto the highway. A truck pulled out, nearly cutting them off, and Cash rode the shoulder to keep from hitting it.

The river loomed ahead. Cash picked up speed. The SUV did the same, but it suddenly swerved as an oncoming car crossed the line. The car zoomed past. The driver of the SUV tried to straighten its course, but it was going too fast and he lost control.

The vehicle skidded, careened to the right, then went into a spin. Instead of coming to a stop, it flipped, then rolled.

Cash muttered a curse, slowed the Cadillac, then threw it into Park on the side of the road.

The SUV dived nose first under the water, the rest of the vehicle slowly sinking.

If Tyler was in there, he might drown.

Déjà vu of losing her son made BJ's head spin. For a moment the world blurred. She was standing on the embankment, watching rescue workers haul her ex-husband's car from the lake.

Panic, fear and sorrow gripped her, and tears blurred her eyes. If she'd been with them, maybe she could have saved her son.

*Dammit, BJ. Get a grip.*

*It might not be too late for Tyler.*

She threw open the door, yanked off her shoes, ran toward the river and dived in.

The current was strong and immediately swept her downstream, but she took a deep breath, swam below and fought it as she searched for the vehicle. The water was muddy and cold, and a chill invaded her as she spotted Cash yanking at the door to the driver's side.

She kicked hard and swam deeper, pushing forward until she reached the other side of the SUV. The murky water blurred her vision, and loose strands of her hair drifted in a tangle around her face. She pushed them away, leaned toward the window and peered inside. No one in the passenger seat.

Heart pounding, she swam to the back window, then pressed her face against it. A child's blanket lay on the seat, a bulge beneath it.

Fear choked her. Was Tyler under that blanket?

CASH PULLED AND yanked at the car door, but it wouldn't budge. One look inside and he'd seen the driver, a dark-clad figure slumped over the wheel. Blood gushing.

No seat belt.

Muddy river water seeped into the car, slowly

filling it and making it impossible to see if any-one else was inside. He spotted a blanket in the back and prayed that if Tyler was under it, he was alive.

He had to get the damn door open. But it wouldn't budge.

The window was his best bet. He ripped off his shirt, wrapped it around his fist, then punched the glass. Nothing happened and he tried again.

The force of the current was too strong.

And his lungs were about to explode.

Suddenly, BJ appeared beside him with a rock in one hand. Hair swirled around her face, and terror widened her eyes. But she shoved the rock toward him.

Adrenaline fueled his strength, and he swung the rock against the glass. It took three tries, but it finally shattered. Water gushed into the SUV, and he fought the current to reach inside and open the car door.

The force of the water threw him backward. BJ

was struggling. He motioned for her to surface for air, but she shook her head.

He didn't have time to argue.

He grabbed the car door, swam to the driver, then yanked the body from the car. The hooded sweatshirt had shrouded the person's face. The body was lighter than he'd expected.

A woman?

He didn't take the time to look. He tucked the body under one arm, desperate to see if Tyler was in the backseat.

BJ must have been thinking the same thing. She fumbled with the seat, trying to move it forward so she could reach in back.

The current tried to sweep her away. He caught her and pushed her forward. She clutched the edge of the door, and he guided her inside.

His heart pounded as she grabbed the blanket.

BJ'S LUNGS STRAINED for air as she dragged the blanket from the seat. Thank God…

Tyler wasn't there.

Relief flooded her but her lungs were about to

explode. She frantically searched the floor, but found nothing.

Cash pulled her from the vehicle and held on to her as they swam upward. As soon as they broke the surface, she gasped for a breath. Cash did the same.

He clutched the driver's body under one arm and motioned for her to swim to shore. She took another breath to get a second wind, then gathered her strength and pumped her legs and arms to propel her to the river's edge. When she reached the embankment, she crawled onto it and collapsed, the soggy blanket clutched in one hand.

Tears blinded her vision, and a sob broke loose. She pressed the blanket to her cheeks, inhaled the little boy's odor blended with the smell of the murky water, and emotions overwhelmed her.

An image of Tyler hugging this blanket for comfort taunted her. Her son had loved his blanket, too. A ratty yellow one that he'd worn thin by rubbing one section of ribbon with his fingers.

Her heart had broken at the thought of him being without it. But she hadn't wanted to part with it, either.

So she'd cut it in half, kept a piece of it under her pillow and buried the remainder with him. She remembered tucking it under his arm the way he'd held it at night, then kissing his cheek as she'd been forced to say goodbye.

Behind her, Cash's grunt brought her back to reality.

Her son was gone, but they still might be able to save Tyler. She prayed the driver of that car was alive and could tell them where he'd left the little boy.

Cash's muscles were straining as he shoved the body onto the dirt. She crawled to them, and he flipped the body over.

All black clothing, black hoodie.

Long strands of hair peeking out. Tangled and wet.

Cash pushed the hood back. BJ gasped again.

Diane.

Sondra's best friend.

Diane had acted so concerned and worried. Elmore had trusted her. Had believed she didn't know where Tyler was.

Sondra would have trusted her, as well.

Which would have made it easy for Diane to get close enough to kill Sondra. Diane would also have known Sondra's routine. Her schedule.

But why would Diane kill her best friend?

Cash checked the woman's pulse. "We need an ambulance."

BJ pushed to her feet, then staggered back toward the Cadillac. She dug her phone from her purse, then punched 911. "We need an ambulance at Stone Gap. A woman ran her car into the river. She's unconscious."

She hung up and rushed back to Cash.

He was on his knees, patting Diane's cheeks in an attempt to rouse her to consciousness. Diane's face looked sickly white. Her clothing was soaked and covered in murk from the river.

A siren wailed.

"Come on, dammit," Cash said. "Wake up and tell us what you did with the boy."

It did no good. Diane didn't move.

She lay stone still, the slight rise and fall of her chest the only indication she was alive.

The ambulance screeched to a stop, lights twirling in the darkness falling over the land.

Land as desolate as BJ felt.

Medics jumped out and ran toward them, then took her vitals. Seconds later they retrieved a stretcher and loaded her onto it.

"Do you know her name?" one of them asked Cash.

"Diane Stuckey," he replied. "I have no idea if she has family."

The medics carried her to the ambulance.

"I'd like to ride with her," Cash said.

"I'm sorry, sir, but that's against the rules. You can follow us."

Irritation darkened Cash's eyes, but he didn't argue. BJ was trembling as she followed him to the Cadillac. His jaw hardened as he started the car and followed the ambulance.

BJ turned to look out the window. Emotions racked her, and she swiped at tears she couldn't stop.

Cash reached out and laid his hand over hers. His palm felt warm and strong, comforting. She held on to it for dear life.

Traffic and night noises blurred into the background. Storm clouds rolled in, making it seem dark and eerie.

She kept seeing her son in that wreck. His face battered and bruised. His still chest… The soul-deep ache that never went away stirred to full force.

Cash's phone buzzed. He snatched it up. "The kidnapper crashed into the river. I'm following the ambulance. Did you catch the shooter?" A pause. "Hell. Just meet us at the hospital."

Cash veered into the hospital parking lot, and they both jumped out and ran toward the ambulance.

But the medic shook his head, his expression grave.

Diane was dead. The shooter had escaped.

And they had no idea if Tyler was dead or alive.

# *Chapter Seventeen*

Frustration built inside Cash.

Diane Stuckey was dead.

Sondra's friend had kidnapped her son and now they had no idea where he was.

Had she hurt Tyler?

And why would she steal her best friend's little boy? Was she jealous of Sondra? Did she want the child for herself?

Or was it all about the money?

"I issued a BOLO for the truck," Maddox said. "Whitefeather is examining the woman's car and searching for a phone. We'll look for a computer at her home. Somewhere in there, we'll find this son of a bitch."

"You got the license plate of the truck?" Cash asked.

Maddox frowned. "Afraid not. We need to know more about Diane."

BJ had excused herself to go to the ladies' room to clean up. She was obviously shaken over the death of Sondra's friend, and they were both still wet from the river. But something else seemed to be bothering her.

She'd looked almost despondent when they'd emerged from the river.

Maddox's phone buzzed. "It's Elmore."

Maddox stepped aside to talk to Elmore and Cash went to the Cadillac to retrieve his shirt. The damn thing was wet but he couldn't do anything about that until they returned to the cabin.

By the time he made it back to the waiting room, BJ had emerged from the ladies' room. She'd combed her hair and wrung some of the water from her clothes, but her face was splotched. She'd been crying.

Cash's gut clenched. "BJ, are you okay?"

She averted her gaze but nodded. "Any word on the shooter?"

"Not yet. Maddox issued a BOLO." He gestured toward Maddox. "He's talking to Elmore now."

"That can't be a pleasant phone call."

"No." Cash touched her elbow gently. "BJ?"

She lifted her chin. "I'm fine, Cash. Let's just focus on finding where Diane might have taken Tyler."

Cash hissed between his teeth. "Right."

Finding Tyler was all that mattered.

Maddox walked toward them, his expression worried. "Brett said Nix has been home all evening, so we can rule him out. Whitefeather's searching Diane's vehicle. Elmore said Diane has no family. I have her address. I'm going to search her house."

"We'll go with you," BJ said.

Maddox shook his head. "This is police business. Besides, you two were almost killed tonight. BJ, you probably have enough now to get the charges dropped against Cash. Focus on that. Go back to the cabin and I'll keep you posted."

"Look, Maddox, we'll be safer with you," Cash said. "If we find Tyler, he's going to need me. I'm not going to let him down again."

BJ FOCUSED ON finding out all she could about Diane Stuckey from the internet as they swung by Horseshoe Creek so she and Cash could change.

Maddox's wife Rose loaned her some jeans and a shirt along with a pair of cowboy boots. Meanwhile, Maddox secured a warrant for Diane's condo, car, computer, phone and her personal belongings. Cash retrieved his truck, and they followed Maddox to Diane's condo.

"Her parents weren't well-off like Elmore, but they tried to give her a good life. She and Sondra became friends when they met at a horseback riding class. Both girls excelled, and went on to show. Diane had to work mucking stalls to help pay for her trainer." She skimmed for more information. "Both girls did well in competition, although Sondra always placed first and Diane second."

"Friends and rivals." Cash made a low sound in his throat. "So Diane could have been jealous of Sondra. She got tired of coming in second."

"It's possible." BJ found some photos Diane had posted of her and Sondra on the first day of college and at dressage award ceremonies. Sondra's father stood beside her, looking regal and important, while one photo caught Diane watching them with envy.

"YOU MIGHT BE RIGHT. Diane may have wanted the life Sondra had." BJ found a photo of Diane holding Tyler at his first birthday party. "Sondra always came in first in everything. She had her father's love, and then her own child."

"But Diane has that expensive condo. Where did she get the money?"

"There are pictures of her with several different men, a couple of them older. She may have had a sugar daddy."

"Then why ask for ransom money?"

"To throw police off of the real motive?" BJ searched Diane's Facebook posts "There are some comments here about Diane having health issues a couple of years ago. I don't think she could get pregnant."

BJ drummed her fingers on her thigh. "If she wanted Sondra's family and loved Tyler, at least she would have taken care of him. She would've left him somewhere safe."

Cash nodded. "What if Tyler was with the shooter, though? Just because Diane wanted Tyler doesn't mean her cohort does."

Cash veered into the complex and parked. They climbed out and met Maddox at the door.

"Cash, you have to stay outside again," Maddox said. "I don't want any evidence thrown out because of your presence."

"Maddox, the fact that you're related to Cash could raise doubts," BJ said.

"Maybe. But you can testify that Cash didn't take part in the search, and that I didn't plant evidence."

Cash hissed in frustration but stepped back. Maddox picked the lock, then pushed the door open.

"Sheriff McCullen here. I have a warrant. Is anyone home?" Maddox called out.

"I think she lived alone," BJ said.

"Let's look around," Maddox said as he went inside.

"What are we searching for?" BJ asked.

Maddox tossed her a pair of latex gloves. "Phone records, personal notes, a calendar, journal, anything to indicate who she was working with."

BJ yanked on the gloves. "I'll check the kitchen."

"I'll take the desk in the den," Maddox said. "BJ, search Diane's bedroom first."

BJ veered down the hallway, once again struck by the plush furnishings. As Cash had said after his initial search earlier that day, there was nothing visible to indicate a child had been here. No toys, children's books, kid's blanket or bedding.

The master held a canopied bed draped in white with a white satin comforter.

She searched the dresser drawers. T-shirts and yoga pants, sexy lingerie.

The pictures on her Facebook page were months old. Did Diane have a recent lover? If so, who was he? Was he involved with this kidnapping plan?

BJ moved to the closet, and found jeans, T-shirts, Western attire, boots and belts. According to her social media sites, Diane gave horseback riding lessons to children at the stable where she'd taken lessons herself.

Maybe someone there knew who Diane was involved with—or someone that could have been her accomplice.

She dug deeper in the closet and found two boxes with designer stilettos, and several cocktail dresses. One side also held a man's pair of work boots and a man's denim duster.

The coat was size 40, the shoes size 11. No business card or ID inside, though.

She ran her fingers along the top of the closet

shelf in search of a journal or calendar, but found nothing. Same with the nightstand drawers. She even checked beneath the mattress. Nothing.

She moved to the master bath and checked the drawers. Basic cosmetics and toiletries.

One toothbrush in the ceramic holder but there was an extra one in the drawer.

A blue one.

The blue one could belong to Diane's male friend.

She plucked it from the holder and carried it to Maddox.

"A man's coat and boots are in the closet. And this toothbrush might belong to Diane's male friend."

Maddox bagged the toothbrush. "I'll send this and her laptop to the lab."

Maddox pushed a sticky-note pad toward BJ. "I found this in the desk. Phone number. No name. I called it and got the voice mail for Hyatt Spillman."

"He worked with Cash at the Triple X," BJ said.

"He claimed Cash was in love with Sondra and that he argued with her the morning she died."

Maddox shifted, his jaw tight. "And he's connected to Diane. He could have been the one who framed Cash."

DISBELIEF CHURNED INSIDE CASH.

Sondra's best friend had betrayed her. And now she might have taken Tyler?

God, he'd never suspected her. She'd acted innocent when they'd questioned her about the little boy's whereabouts.

BJ joined him outside and explained about finding Spillman's number in Diane's condo. Had that bastard set him up?

Maddox clenched his phone in his hand as he stepped out of the condo. "Whitefeather just called. He found some discrepancies in Elmore's financials. He also had a life insurance policy on Tyler. I'm going to question Elmore again."

The possibility that Sondra's father might have been part of this mess made Cash curse. "We'll find Spillman."

Maddox gave him a warning look. "Wait, Cash, I'm running this show."

BJ cleared her throat. "Maddox, if he has Tyler, he might be panicking. We need to get to him before he disappears completely."

Maddox looked torn, but finally agreed. "Just don't do anything rash. If he's at home, just watch him. Let me know and I'll be right there."

Cash wrangled his temper under control, then lifted his fingers in a Scout's pledge. "Yes, sir."

The clouds darkened, hovering above, threatening rain. A stiff wind picked up, swirling dried tumbleweed and dust, a reminder of Wyoming's dust storms as Cash drove toward the Triple X.

BJ checked her watch. "Tyler should be home in his bed right now."

The pain in her voice twisted Cash's insides. "So should you, BJ. Let me take you back to the cabin. You've done enough for me already."

"No," BJ said. "I'm not giving up until we bring Tyler home safe."

BJ bit down on her lip and turned to look out

the window. A second later, a tear seeped from her eye and trickled down her cheek.

He wanted to comfort her, ask her why this case was getting to her. But hell, she probably just had a soft spot for kids, like he did.

That alone made him worry about her.

God, he'd already lost one friend this week. He didn't want to care about BJ, but he was starting to. And he couldn't live with the guilt if something bad happened to her.

Nerves on edge, he turned onto the road that led to the Triple X. A sliver of moonlight glowed across the pasture. Horses galloped and cattle grazed on the hill. Donovan's truck was parked in front of the farmhouse, but they passed it and parked at the bunkhouses.

At this time of night, most of the ranch hands had turned in. Work started at first light. Spillman's rusted truck was parked sideways by the bunkhouse.

BJ touched his arm before he climbed out. "Remember what Maddox said, Cash. We just need to see if he's here."

An engine rumbled in the quiet as he slid from the truck. Cash scanned the surrounding area in search of trouble. Car lights flickered across the terrain in the distance and disappeared over a hill.

BJ started toward the bunkhouse, but Cash had a bad feeling. The bunkhouse door was ajar.

He caught BJ's arm and motioned for her to stay behind him. If Spillman was involved in this mess, that meant he'd tried to kill them.

He was damned tired of sitting on the sidelines and letting Maddox and BJ put themselves in the line of fire for him.

The hair on the back of his neck prickled as he inched forward. Wind whistled through the wood slats. He hesitated, pausing to listen for someone inside.

Nothing.

Still, Spillman could have seen them coming and be hiding, waiting to ambush him.

BJ followed on his heels, but he held his arm out to keep her from entering, then glanced through the door. His chest clenched at the sight of blood on the floor.

*"Wait,"* he mouthed to BJ.

He crept inside, then came to an abrupt halt. More blood.

Dammit. Spillman couldn't help them. He was dead.

# *Chapter Eighteen*

"Is he in there?" BJ whispered from the doorway.

"Stay there," Cash growled. He quickly scanned the adjoining bath, but no one was inside. It appeared that no one was using the second bedroom, either.

The room and Spillman's body needed to be searched, but he couldn't contaminate the scene or Maddox would be furious.

He urged BJ away from the bunkhouse. "Spillman's dead. I have to call Maddox."

BJ's eyes widened, but she nodded and straightened, then began scouring the area. Cash pressed Maddox's number. The phone rang three times before he answered.

"Sheriff McCullen."

"It's Cash. We're at Spillman's bunk. He's dead. Gunshot to the chest."

Maddox muttered a sound of frustration. "Don't touch anything. I'll be there ASAP and I'll call a crime unit."

"How's Elmore?" Cash asked.

"Distraught, but Jasper was there for support. He says he can explain the financial discrepancies. Says his accountant's assistant skimmed money from him. He fired both of them six months ago.

"Whitefeather verified his story. The accountant moved to Texas and took the assistant with him. Apparently they were an item."

"What about the life insurance on Tyler?"

"His lawyer advised him to do that for Sondra's sake. I asked the lab to put a rush on the DNA on the toothbrush and compare it to Spillman's." He paused. "I'm on my way. Jasper was going to hang around and make sure Elmore was safe in case the kidnapper came after him. We'll need to talk to everyone on the Triple X."

Maddox hung up, and Cash surveyed the hill where the car lights had been. Could the person driving that vehicle be their shooter?

"Were there any signs Tyler had been in that bunk?" BJ asked.

Cash shook his head, then headed toward Spillman's rusty truck. He wanted to search it himself.

But he forced himself not to touch it. Instead, he paced the yard and waited on Maddox.

FATIGUE PULLED AT BJ as Maddox and the crime unit arrived. She and Cash were once again delegated to watching. She sensed it was hardest for Cash—he'd grown up depending on himself, not on others.

One of the team found an envelope of cash inside Spillman's truck.

"Fifteen thousand," Maddox said as he counted the bills.

"Could be payment for his part in the kidnapping," Cash suggested.

"Or it could be savings from his job," Maddox said. "We need more proof."

The ranch owner, Wilson Donovan, showed up looking harried and upset. "I can't believe he died here on the ranch." The man removed his hat and slapped it against his thigh. "Nothing like this has ever happened to me." He shot Cash a questioning look. "You know what's going on, Koker, you better fess up."

"I'm sorry, sir." Cash squared his shoulders. "It looks like Spillman was involved in Sondra Elmore's death and with her son's disappearance."

"We need to speak to all the ranch hands and employees," Maddox said. "Ask them to meet me in the dining hall in half an hour."

Donovan checked his watch. "It's ten o'clock at night, Sheriff. Can't it wait till tomorrow?"

"No," Maddox replied. "A man was murdered here this evening. Questioning everyone on the ranch as soon as possible is imperative. Whoever shot Spillman could still be on the property."

Donovan's eyes widened in alarm. "All right, I'll make some phone calls."

"Mr. Donovan," Cash said. "I saw a vehicle

driving in the distance on the property when I arrived. I think it might have been a Jeep."

Donovan grunted. "Several of the hands drive Jeeps. What color was it?"

Cash jammed his hands in the pockets of his jeans. "Couldn't tell. It was too far away."

Donovan grunted again, then gripped his cell phone and stepped back to his truck to make the call.

"He blames me for bringing trouble to his place," Cash said, his voice full of regret.

"This isn't your fault, Cash." BJ squeezed his arm. "Hang in there. We'll find out who framed you and bring Tyler home safely."

"What if we don't?" The agony in Cash's voice tugged at her heartstrings.

She couldn't resist. She took both his hands in hers and cradled them against her chest. "We will, Cash. You have my word."

CASH DESPERATELY WANTED to believe BJ, but anxiety knotted every muscle in his body. He felt helpless as he watched Maddox and Deputy

Whitefeather question the ranch hands and other employees.

"Listen, guys, one of your ranch hands, Hyatt Spillman, was murdered in his room," Maddox said. "We believe Diane Stuckey and Spillman conspired to kill Sondra Elmore and kidnap her son."

Shocked gasps and murmurs followed.

"We found a large sum of cash in Spillman's truck," Maddox continued. "If you know where he got the money, please come forward. Any information will be helpful."

A hand Cash recognized as a new hire named Jordan stepped up and approached Whitefeather. Cash stood a safe distance away, but the condemning looks from the other men suggested they thought he was behind the trouble on the ranch.

BJ coaxed him outside, and he paced the porch as the interrogations continued.

"Maddox is looking for gun residue on the workers' hands," BJ said.

Meanwhile, the sun had faded hours ago, and the clock was ticking, precious time slipping by.

Midnight struck as Maddox and Whitefeather finished and joined them on the porch. One by one, the men headed back to their bunks to get some shut-eye before the sun signaled another day on the ranch.

Across the way, the ambulance was pulling away, transporting Spillman's body to the morgue for an autopsy.

Maddox approached him and BJ. "One of the hands said Spillman was a gambler, that he might have been in debt."

"So he needed money," Cash said.

Maddox nodded. "We'll verify the information. Unfortunately, no one saw anyone hanging around tonight."

Whitefeather cleared his throat. "One guy said he'd seen Diane with Spillman. Said they looked as if they were arguing. Later, he asked Spillman, but he said it was nothing. That Diane was just moody."

Cash balled his hands into fists. Dammit, they

needed more. Something concrete to lead them to where Tyler was being held.

"There's not much we can do tonight," Maddox said, his voice tired. "Maybe DNA, phone records or financials will turn up something in the morning. Jasper said he asked the media to keep running Tyler's picture on the news. Maybe someone will spot him and call in."

The hope he tried to inject into his voice fell flat. Maddox looked as frustrated as Cash was.

"Everyone get some rest. I'll keep you posted."

Cash hesitated. He didn't want to give up tonight.

How could he sleep, knowing Tyler was still missing and that two people associated with his kidnapping were dead?

BJ'S HEART FELT heavy as Cash dropped her at the cabin on Horseshoe Creek. The day had been a nightmare.

Memories of almost being killed and diving into that river in search of Tyler would probably keep her awake all night.

Cash looked tortured, too—which made her even more determined to clear his name. She had a basis now to get the charges dropped.

But all he cared about was Tyler.

Cash insisted on searching the cabin to make sure the shooter wasn't hiding inside, waiting to attack. When he cleared the space, he returned to her in the living room. She stood by the window, looking out at the night. A few lone stars glittered through the clouds, the moon barely a sliver. The sky looked gray and just as gloomy as BJ felt.

"You all right?" Cash asked gruffly.

"Yes, are you?" She lifted her hand and brushed it across his cheek. He sucked in a sharp breath.

She'd vowed never to get involved with a client. Not to trust any man.

Except…how could she resist this sexy, strong man?

She looked up into Cash's eyes and was moved by his tenderness. Desperate for his touch, for comfort, she pressed her hand over his chest. Beneath her palm, his heart pounded, strong and alive.

He sucked in a sharp breath, the hunger radiating from him stirring her own. How long had it been since she'd slept with a man? Since someone strong and caring had held her?

He brushed her hair from her cheek. "BJ?"

"Shh, just hold me for a minute."

He made a low sound in his throat as if he was struggling not to touch her. Then his eyes darkened, and he pulled her up against him.

BJ leaned into him, savoring the strength and safety in his big, powerful muscles. He rubbed her back gently, soothing her, stroking away her anxiety and arousing a part of her she thought was dead.

The need to be with a man, to be intimate. To feel his love erasing the heartache that would never leave her.

"Talk to me," Cash murmured. "Today was rough. But something else is wrong. I can feel it."

She swallowed hard. She couldn't make her voice work.

Instead she lifted her head and gazed into his eyes. Dark, soulful, tinged with the pain of his past and his worry over Tyler.

And his need to prove himself innocent. Maybe to prove he was worthy of being a McCullen.

"I don't want to talk," she whispered.

She cradled his face between her hands, rose on tiptoes and pressed her mouth to his.

He stiffened, his hands gripping her arms as if to set her away from him. She refused to let him.

She needed him.

Her emotions mingling with desire, she traced her tongue along the seam of his lips until he opened for her. She teased his mouth and drove her hands through his thick hair, deepening the kiss.

With a low growl in his throat, he finally gave in and plunged his tongue into her mouth. Their tongues met, thrust for thrust, a dance of need and hunger and a longing so strong that she lowered her hands to stroke the hard planes of his back.

His hands moved, as well, dragging her into

the V of his thighs, settling her against his thick, hard sex. Erotic sensations spiraled inside her, creating a slow burn that made her tear at the buttons of his shirt.

One button popped open, then another, and she raked the fabric back to press a kiss to his bare chest. He gripped her arms, threw his head back and moaned.

"God, BJ..."

Emboldened by the depth of his desire, she spread kisses all along his chest, touching scars from injuries that must have been traumatic, scars that aroused protective feelings for the man.

His fingers tangled in her hair and he tilted her head back, then planted kisses along her neck and throat.

She wanted more.

So did he.

They frantically kissed again, whispered longing in each stroke, and he walked her backward toward the sofa. She allowed him to push her onto it, but she refused to release him.

Instead she teased him again by stroking his

chest and lowering her hands to his hips. He grunted and reached for the bottom of her shirt. Then he climbed on top of her, straddling her hips as he lifted the shirt over her head. He tossed it to the side, but it hit a picture frame, and the frame fell onto the table.

Cash reached sideways to right it, then went very still.

BJ held her breath, need mingling with the realization that the picture he was looking at was of her lost son.

"BJ?" His eyes searched hers. "You're married? You have a family?"

Sadness choked her. She didn't want to talk about her loss. She wanted to feel his hands on her, making her forget.

He angled his head in question and set the picture back on the table. Questions darkened his expressive eyes. "Answer me."

"I was divorced," she said. "I…lost my son."

He muttered a low curse. "How?"

"A car accident." In spite of her resolve to control her emotions, tears choked her voice.

His posture stiffened, anger and frustration twisting his expression, and he lifted his body from hers.

She reached for him again. “Cash, please.”

He cleared his throat. “I’ve done a lot of things I’m not proud of in my day, BJ.” He lowered his mouth and dropped a tender kiss on her forehead. “But I don’t want making love to you to be one of them.”

Without another word, he walked toward the door. When it closed behind him, the tears she’d been fighting spilled over.

# *Chapter Nineteen*

BJ wanted to run after Cash.

But his words echoed in her head. He didn't want to regret making love to her. Which meant he would regret it.

So would she.

At least he'd had the good sense to put a stop to their frenzied behavior.

She picked up her son's photo, stared at his sweet little face and then hugged it to her chest.

Making love with Cash might have temporarily assuaged the anguish, but it would always be there.

She couldn't allow herself to feel anything for Cash. Loving someone meant agony when they were gone. Cash wasn't even a free man. He was a cowboy struggling to find his place and clear his name.

Worse, he was her client.

She swiped at her tears, walked to the bathroom and washed her face, then slipped into pajamas. Exhausted, she crawled into bed and tried to banish the memory of Cash's hands touching her.

But when she closed her eyes, she felt his arms wrap around her. She savored that comforting feeling.

For one moment in time, she'd felt wanted. Almost loved, as if she deserved it, when for the last two years she'd known she didn't. That she was broken after her son died, and she'd never be whole again.

But the sound of the wind beating a tree branch against the windowpane made her jerk her eyes open and face reality.

She glanced at the window to make sure the shooter hadn't found her.

Then she reminded herself that Cash was next door, plus Maddox had security on the ranch.

Sondra's murderer and Tyler's kidnapper would have to be pretty ballsy to come after her or Cash on the sheriff's property.

She was safe here tonight. But she was alone.

And she worried she always would be.

PERSPIRATION BEADED CASH'S neck as he climbed the steps to the porch of his cabin. Before he entered, he stared at the sprawling ranch land. Horseshoe Creek.

He'd never imagined staying here, much less being a part of it and the family it belonged to.

The light in BJ's cabin went out, and he realized she was probably going to bed.

Dammit, it had taken every ounce of his strength to walk away from her. He wanted her more than he'd ever wanted any woman in his life.

The anguish in her eyes tore him up inside. She'd had a child.

A little boy. But she'd lost him.

He wanted to know the story, yet he'd left before she could explain because...because why?

He didn't want to know. Didn't want to hear the despair in her voice or her sad story. Didn't want to get close to her or care.

*You already do, fool.*

All the more reason to keep his distance—at least emotionally. Which meant he wouldn't touch her again.

Hopefully, they'd find Tyler and end this case soon. Then she'd go back to her life. Her father was a well-known attorney, prestigious.

She was completely out of Cash's league.

He didn't fit here on Horseshoe Creek, and he sure as hell didn't fit with BJ Alexander.

The wind rustled the trees, the dark clouds hovering. Exhausted, but too antsy to sleep, he stepped inside the cabin and turned on the television. A news segment was airing.

Tyler's picture appeared on the screen, with a plea for anyone who had information regarding his disappearance to call the tip line at the sheriff's department. NCMEC, the National Center for Missing and Exploited Children, had been looped in and a nationwide Amber Alert issued.

Elmore had agreed to pay the ransom.

*He* had made the drop. But it had been a setup. The kidnapper had never intended to return Tyler.

It made sense that Diane might want the little boy, but whoever had him now might hurt him or get rid of him.

Cash studied the photograph of Tyler with a pang in his chest. That afternoon, he'd taught Tyler how to play T-ball in the yard, while Sondra went riding with a friend. Tyler's laugh still echoed in his ears, then his shout of joy when he'd hit the ball.

The picture of BJ's son flashed in his mind's eye. He didn't know how old he would have been if he'd lived, but in the picture she kept on the end table, he looked to be about three. Tyler's age.

No wonder it had hit her so hard when she'd seen that car fly into the river.

Cash flipped off the television, found a beer in the fridge and popped the top. One sip and he stretched out on the sofa with his phone in his hand. He needed sleep, but he needed answers worse.

And he needed to know BJ was safe.

With one ear cocked for sounds of trouble, he closed his eyes. “I’m going to bring you home, Tyler,” he promised.

BJ’s sweet scent lingered on his skin, tormenting him.

But he would keep his hands off BJ.

THE SOUND OF her phone buzzing with a text woke BJ. She’d tossed and turned and dreamed about her son most of the night.

Her heart ached this morning.

She had had the same dream over and over. She and Aaron were playing or singing or hiking, then she tucked him in bed, only to wake up the next morning and find he was gone. That his little bed would never hold him again, and she would never see his little smile again or hear his precious voice.

She brushed at more tears, then her phone buzzed with a text.

DNA tests on the toothbrush found at Diane's matches Cash's. We need to talk.

BJ bolted out of bed. Cash had said he'd met Diane, but he hadn't mentioned they were involved.

Had he lied about their relationship?

He'd seemed shocked to find out she was driving that car and that she was involved in the kidnapping.

Because he'd slept with her?

A SECOND TEXT came in seconds later. Also from Maddox.

Get Cash and meet me at the house for breakfast. Will drive to the lab from there. The analyst has more information on DNA and Tyler's father. She wants to deliver the news face-to-face.

BJ texted Okay, then texted Cash to be ready in half an hour to meet Maddox. Then she jumped in the shower. She needed to be fresh and alert when she saw Cash. Needed to wipe the scent of his kisses off her.

And forget that she'd almost made love with him.

Had he played her for a fool so she wouldn't see his playboy side?

Irritated that she'd lost her objectivity, she rinsed and dried off, then pulled her hair back into a low bun at the nape of her neck.

A minute later, a knock sounded. She hurried to answer and found Cash standing on the porch. In spite of her resolve to remain detached, her breath caught as his big masculine body filled the doorway.

His gaze raked over her, then he set his jaw with a scowl. He must regret the night before as much as she did. "Maddox has something?" he asked in a deep voice.

"DNA results. We're having breakfast at the house, then going to the lab. The analyst wants to talk to us."

Cash climbed in his truck and drove to the farmhouse. As they entered, the homey scents of maple syrup, pancakes and bacon filled the air, making BJ's stomach growl.

Mama Mary greeted them with hot coffee and ushered them to the dining room, where she'd set out the food buffet-style.

Cash hung back, obviously still uncomfortable with the McCullens.

"Help yourself," Maddox said. "Rose is feeding the baby or she'd be down."

She took a plate and filled it, then Maddox and Cash did the same. An awkward quiet settled over the room.

"What's the news?" Cash asked.

"The analyst has DNA results that she needs to talk to us about." Maddox stabbed a piece of bacon and munched on it.

"What's wrong?" Cash asked. "I saw that look between you two. Do you know something you're not telling me?"

Maddox worked his mouth from side to side.

"DNA on the toothbrush we found at Diane's belongs to you, Cash."

Cash dropped his fork with a clatter. "What?"

"I thought you weren't involved with Diane," BJ said.

Cash straightened in the chair. "I wasn't. I mean, I met her a couple of times when she was with Sondra, but we never spent any time together."

Maddox pinned him with a questioning stare. "Then how do you explain your DNA on a toothbrush in her bathroom?"

CASH FORCED HIMSELF not to react, when he wanted to punch a wall.

He had no explanation for the toothbrush. "I have no idea. Someone must have placed it there to frame me."

"Just like they put you in that motel with Sondra's body?" Maddox asked.

Cash ground his teeth at the doubt in BJ's eyes. That hurt the most. He thought he'd finally convinced her of his innocence. "I know it sounds crazy, but until we went there, I'd never been in Diane's condo, much less her bathroom."

BJ set her coffee cup on the table. "Setting you up like that took planning."

Cash scraped a hand through his hair in frustration. "Damn right it did. And I want to know who did it."

"Let's find out what Devon has to say. She's our lead analyst." Maddox polished off his coffee, then stood.

Cash pushed aside his plate. "Then what are we waiting for?"

Mama Mary popped her head in. "Y'all want seconds?"

"No, thanks, we have to go," Maddox said.

"Thanks for breakfast," Cash said with a tentative smile.

BJ wiped her mouth, then placed the gingham napkin on the table. "It was delicious. We appreciate the meal."

Mama Mary gushed, "Anytime! I love cooking for my boys."

Cash swallowed hard. She meant Maddox, Brett and Ray. Or was she including him?

Sun slanted through the trees as they veered onto the highway. The memory of the night before tormented Cash.

Whatever trust he'd gained with BJ had evaporated.

"I'm sorry about your son," he said, remembering the anguish in her eyes when he'd found that photo. "What happened, BJ?"

Her sharp intake of breath vibrated with raw grief. "I don't want to talk about it."

Cash had a dozen questions about her and the man she'd married and lost, and about her child, but her statement made him clamp his mouth shut. She had her right to privacy. After all, she was his lawyer, not his friend.

Or…lover.

He had to remember it.

Although seeing her in those tight jeans and cowboy boots stirred his hunger for her.

He parked next to Maddox, and the three of them entered the county lab together. Maddox led them down a corridor to a small office with windows that overlooked one of the labs.

An attractive brunette named Devon Squires introduced herself.

"You have news?" Maddox asked, cutting to the chase.

Devon tapped a set of papers on her desk, then nodded. "First of all, I told you the DNA on the toothbrush belongs to Mr. Koker."

"Yes," Maddox said.

The need to defend himself hit Cash. He opened his mouth to argue, but Devon held up a warning finger. "Let me finish. There's more."

"Were there fingerprints?" Maddox asked.

Devon consulted another file. "Actually, we found Diane's prints and a partial print but it didn't belong to Mr. Koker."

"Whose were they?" Maddox asked.

"I haven't identified them yet, but if we find a suspect, I can compare."

Cash knotted his hands in his lap. Not finding his prints was a good sign.

"You sounded excited, as if you had a lead," Maddox said.

"I do," Devon said. "After analyzing Mr. Koker's DNA, I determined he is not Tyler Elmore's father."

"I told you I wasn't," Cash said.

"There's something else," Devon said. "We ran Tyler's DNA in search of his father, and got a hit."

Cash's pulse jumped. "You know who his father is?"

"No, the hit wasn't for the father."

"I don't understand," Maddox said.

"That's the kicker," Devon replied. "Tyler's DNA was a familial match to another child in the system."

"That's impossible," Cash said. "Sondra only had one child."

"That's true. The match didn't belong to Sondra," Devon said. "Actually, the common genetic markers point to the fact that both children share the same father. I looked at an electronic version of the child's birth certificate and, just like Tyler's, you're listed as this child's father."

"You have a child?" BJ asked, her voice cracking.

Cash shook his head in confusion. "No. That's a mistake."

"Yes, it is," Devon said. "Neither Tyler nor this child shares your DNA, Mr. Koker."

"Then someone *is* framing Cash," Maddox said.

Devon smiled. "It certainly appears that way."

"Where is this child?" BJ asked. "Why was his or her DNA in the system?"

A frown tugged at Devon's eyes. "It's a little boy. He's five years old," she said. "His DNA is in the system because he's on a list for a kidney transplant."

Cash took a deep breath. "The child's condition must be serious."

"It is," Devon said. "He needs a donor match ASAP. A family member would be best."

"But Tyler's too little," BJ said.

"What about the little boy's mother?" Maddox asked.

Devon breathed deeply. "His mother was murdered."

Shock waves rolled through Cash. Tyler and the boy were half brothers. Both boys' mothers were murdered.

Were the two cases connected?

# *Chapter Twenty*

BJ's mind spun with questions.

When she'd first heard the boy's birth certificate listed Cash as his father, doubt had filled her.

But DNA didn't lie. Cash wasn't Tyler's father or this other child's. But someone had intentionally listed his name on the other child's birth certificate.

Who? And why lie?

To set up Cash and protect the boy's real father.

"Who was the little boy's mother?" Maddox asked.

Devon read from the file. "A woman named Frannie Cooper. She used to live in Cheyenne and worked as a hairstylist. She died when her son, Drew, was two. She had no family, so Drew went into the foster system."

"God," Cash said. "Poor kid."

Just like Cash had. Only he had family—he just hadn't known it. Tyler didn't know about Drew, either.

"He was never adopted?" BJ asked.

"No." Devon shook her head. "He got sick about a year ago. He needs that kidney transplant."

"What about his foster family?" Cash asked.

"They turned him back into the system, said they couldn't take care of an ill child, not with a handful of others in their house. So far they haven't found a match," Devon answered.

"Did the police arrest anyone for Frannie's murder?" Maddox asked.

Devon shook her head. "No."

"That was three years ago," BJ said. "Do you think her murder is connected to Sondra's?"

"It seems coincidental that both boys' mothers were murdered." Cash drummed his fingers on his thigh. "Maybe Drew's father didn't want his name revealed, just like he didn't want it disclosed that Tyler was his son."

"We have to consider the possibility that Drew's father may not even know about him," Devon said.

"True," BJ said. "But I don't buy it. It makes more sense that he's the one who put Cash's name on the birth certificate."

Maddox snapped his fingers. "Devon, get an official copy of Drew's birth certificate and analyze it to make sure it wasn't altered."

"I'm on it," Devon agreed. "If the father does know about Drew and he knows Drew is sick, maybe he thought he could use the ransom money to pay for the treatment, maybe even pay to get Drew bumped up on the transplant list."

"Let's go to the hospital," BJ said. "If the father has visited or made inquiries about the transplant, one of the nurses or a staff member might be able to ID him."

"Why don't you and Cash pursue that angle," Maddox suggested. "I'll consult with the sheriff who investigated Frannie's death."

Devon nodded. "Meanwhile I'll get hold of that birth certificate and tackle Sondra's computer."

Maddox stood. "Keep me posted."

BJ made to follow Cash out to the truck. She was anxious to talk to the nurses at the hospital and meet this little boy, Drew.

The poor little guy was sick and must feel all alone.

"THERE'S ONE MORE THING," Devon said before everyone could leave.

Cash frowned, bracing himself for more bad news.

Maddox shifted, his expression solemn. "What?"

"The DNA from Cash—was positive." She smiled at Cash. "You're a McCullen. You share the same mother and father as Maddox."

His breath left Cash in a rush. A dozen emotions flickered across Maddox's face. He turned to Cash with an odd look.

Cash didn't know what to expect, but the tough-as-nails sheriff jerked him into a bear hug.

"Good God, all these years we didn't know you even existed." Maddox's voice thickened. "I'm sorry, man. We would have looked for you, found you sooner."

Cash's chest swelled with unexpected pleasure, a feeling he'd never felt before. He had a family. A real family.

Brothers. Sisters-in-law. Nephews.

He even had a surrogate mother in Mama Mary.

"I'm just sorry as hell that Mama and Daddy died without knowing we found you," Maddox said.

Cash slapped Maddox on the back. "I can't believe it. I...never thought I had any family." At least none that wanted him.

But he choked back those words.

Getting close, expecting things from family, not disappointing them—it all came with the territory.

He'd lived his life not having to please anyone.

Sure, it had been lonely as hell, but he'd survived.

Maddox wiped at his eyes. "I have to let Ray and Brett know."

"Let's clear my name first," he said. He couldn't face the disappointment or disapproval in their eyes if somehow he wound up going back to jail.

Maddox studied him for a long minute. "All right. But we are going to clear you, Cash. And we're going to find your twin. He's one of us, too."

One of us? Cash had never been one of anything before. Not a family or a couple.

Dammit, he wanted both. To be a McCullen and to have BJ by his side.

The thought terrified him to the core, and he headed to the door. They had people to talk to about this other kid.

Drew, a little boy who'd been in foster care like him. A child who had a brother he knew nothing about.

They would fix that. They'd find that little boy a kidney.

Once he was well and Tyler was home, maybe Elmore would take them both in.

COMPASSION FILLED BJ. Cash was a McCullen.

In the midst of being framed for murder, he'd found a family. *His* family.

One he'd been torn from years ago.

And not just a family, but a respected one with a successful working ranch and a reputation for being fair and honorable.

Cash parked at the hospital, then cut the engine and rubbed a hand over his face.

"Are you all right?" BJ asked softly.

When he glanced at her, he looked torn.

"I don't know what to do," he said in a gruff voice.

"What do you mean?" she asked softly. "The McCullens are good people. They want you."

His brow wrinkled. "What if I disappoint them?"

BJ couldn't resist; she brushed his cheek with her fingers. "You won't, Cash. All you have to do is be yourself."

A heartbeat passed. "How do you know that? I told you, I've done things I'm not proud of."

She smiled slowly. "You willingly put your life

in danger to save Tyler and me," BJ said. "You're tough and strong, and you're fighting to find a lost little boy. That's admirable."

He leaned into her hand. "I'm nobody's hero, BJ."

"You're Tyler's," she whispered. "Now, let's see if the hospital staff knows anything about Drew's father." She and Cash climbed out and walked up the sidewalk together. "What if Spillman was Tyler's father?" BJ asked. "Did you ever see the two of them together?"

"No," Cash answered. "Like I said, she dropped Tyler off a few times, but we didn't spend much time together the last couple of years."

They stopped at the front desk to inquire about Drew. "Where is he?" BJ asked.

"He's on the third floor in the children's wing," the receptionist said.

"How's he doing?" Cash asked.

The woman's face fell. "He's hanging in there. But I'm not at liberty to discuss his condition."

Frustration knotted BJ's insides. "I understand. Maybe we could talk to the social worker in charge of Drew's case."

She raised a brow. "How did you find out about Drew?"

BJ leaned over the counter separating them from the woman. "We've been working with Sheriff Maddox McCullen on a case that may involve him."

The woman's eyes widened. "I know Sheriff McCullen. He's a good man."

"Yes, he is," BJ said. "Has Drew had any visitors since he was admitted?"

The woman looked down at her computer for a moment.

"It's important," BJ said. "We're trying to find this missing child—"

"Are you talking about Tyler Elmore, the little boy on the news?" she asked.

BJ nodded.

The woman inhaled sharply. "Let me get the director." She paged Dr. Ingles, then made a quick phone call.

Heels clicked on the hard floor, then a middle-aged woman with a dark bob appeared. She spoke to the receptionist, then joined them. "I'm Dr. Ingles. You're inquiring about one of our patients?"

"Yes, the child named Drew. Can we go somewhere private to talk?" BJ said.

Dr. Ingles nodded. "Let me tell the social worker to meet us." She sent a text, then led them to her office.

When the social worker arrived, Dr. Ingles introduced the twentysomething young woman, whose name was Candace Winterbottom.

"Why do you want to know about Drew?" Dr. Ingles asked.

BJ explained the situation. "Tests confirm that Tyler Elmore and Drew are half brothers. With both boys' mothers being murdered, we're working the theory that the two murders are related."

Dr. Ingles and Candace exchanged concerned looks. "Is Drew in danger?" Dr. Ingles asked.

BJ hesitated. "I don't think so," she said. "But the father is a common denominator. We need to know his identity."

"Did you check the birth certificate?" Dr. Ingles asked.

"Yes, but DNA proves the man listed is not Drew's father," BJ said. "We thought he might have visited Drew."

Candace shook her head. "Drew hasn't had any company."

BJ's heart swelled with sympathy for Drew. "How about inquiries into his condition?"

Sadness tinged the woman's eyes. "No inquiries. No relatives or friends of the mother's. No offers to be tested for a DNA match."

"Perhaps his father doesn't know about him," Dr. Ingles suggested. "That happens more than you'd think."

"That's possible," BJ said. Although she had a bad feeling Drew's father did know about him.

And that he'd killed Drew's mother because he didn't want to be exposed.

BJ and Cash followed Candace to Drew's room. The little boy's face looked pale against his dark brown hair. IVs and other tubes helped provide medicine and fluids, but it was clear he wasn't well.

Candace padded across the room to his hospital bed and gently raked his hair from his forehead. Cash stood ramrod straight in the doorway as if his feet were frozen in place.

BJ's heart melted. She crossed the room and stood beside Candace. Slowly, Drew opened his eyes. They were as green as the grass in the pastures on Horseshoe Creek. Did his mother or father have green eyes?

"Drew, you have a visitor," Candace said in a low voice.

Drew's eyes widened. "Someone came to see me?"

"Yes." Candace gave BJ a warning smile. BJ understood the silent message. She couldn't give the child false hope.

Still, she squeezed his limp little hand in hers.

Who in the world could be so cold to take a mother away from a child?

She would have done anything to save her son.

Worse, what kind of a man wouldn't help his own little boy when he needed a kidney to live?

CASH'S HEART ACHED for the kid. Drew reminded him of himself.

He'd been sickly the first three years of his life, and no one had wanted him.

At least his illness hadn't been life-threatening. He'd suffered from asthma and an underdeveloped lung, but he'd outgrown both.

Drew had nobody.

Cash didn't know what he could do, but he would see about changing that once they found the child's damn father.

BJ leaned close to the boy, talking in a low voice. That fancy lawyer he'd thought was stuffy was full of surprises.

She'd shocked him with her passion the night before.

And now…the tenderness in her eyes told him exactly what kind of mother she'd been.

And would be in the future.

*Don't go there.*

*You don't have your life together enough to even think about a relationship with BJ Alexander.*

What did he have to offer a woman like her, anyway?

Cash's phone buzzed. Maddox. "It's Cash," he said as he punched Connect.

"Where are you?" Maddox asked without preamble.

"At the hospital. We met Drew and spoke to the social worker. No one has inquired about him."

"Damn," Maddox said. "Listen, Deputy Whitefeather just called. Elmore somehow slipped out but we've got a trace on his phone. He received another ransom call, Cash. He's on his way to meet the kidnapper."

"I thought Jasper was with him," Cash said.

"He had to leave," Maddox replied.

"How did Elmore get the money so fast?"

"I don't know, but he could be walking into an ambush. I'm twenty minutes out, but on my way."

"Text me the GPS coordinates," Cash said.

Maddox did, and Cash glanced at the map. "I

can be there in ten minutes." He rushed back to the room to tell BJ he was leaving.

She gave Drew a hug. "I'll be back, sweetie. Hang in there, okay?"

"Okay." The kid hugged her with arms so frail they looked like they might break.

They rushed outside, barreled from the parking lot and flew toward the river. Trees swayed in the wind as they neared the section of land where the river forked. Cash slowed and rolled to a stop. He'd hike in on foot and hide while waiting.

A gunshot rent the air.

"Stay put!" He grabbed his pistol from behind the seat, jumped out of the truck and darted through the trees.

Another gunshot, and he spotted Elmore.

Dammit to hell. The man was lying on the embankment, his hand over his chest, blood oozing through his fingers.

# *Chapter Twenty-One*

Cash quickly scanned the area near Elmore, and saw a figure darting up the hill on the opposite side of the river. He wanted to go after him.

But Elmore was bleeding.

Leaves rustled nearby. “I heard gunshots,” BJ said, as she came up behind him.

“Elmore’s hit,” Cash said. “Call an ambulance. And get something to help stop the bleeding.”

Cash jogged toward Elmore. His heart pounded as he scanned the hill where the shooter had disappeared. A car engine fired up in the distance, too far away for him to make it in time.

Dammit.

Elmore lay motionless, eyes closed, his bloody

hand pressed over his chest. Cash checked for a pulse. Barely there, but Elmore was breathing.

He patted the man's face. "Mr. Elmore, who shot you?"

Elmore groaned, and his eyelids fluttered as if he was struggling to open them, but failed.

Footsteps crunched the dry earth. "Cash?"

"He's alive, but in bad shape. The ambulance?"

"On its way." She pressed a cloth to Elmore's wound.

"Elmore," Cash said again "Who did this to you?"

Elmore moaned again, and mumbled something, but Cash couldn't understand him.

A siren wailed, and BJ ran up the hill to meet the ambulance. Another siren followed, blue lights twirling and streaking the cloudy sky as Maddox approached.

Seconds later, Maddox and the medics scrambled down the hill. That damned Sheriff Jasper was on his heels.

"What the hell happened?" Jasper shouted.

The medics checked Elmore's vitals, tossed the bloody cloth aside and applied blood stoppers.

"When I got here, I heard gunshots." Cash pointed toward the right. "The shooter escaped up there. I heard the car take off but Elmore needed help."

"I told him to call me if he received another ransom demand. He should have let me go." Sheriff Jasper wiped sweat from the back of his neck. "What are you doing here anyway, Koker? Did you shoot him?"

Cash's temper rose. "No, I was with BJ."

"BJ?" Jasper asked.

Cash realized he'd used her first name. "My lawyer. She can verify my story."

"It's true," BJ said. "Cash tried to save Mr. Elmore."

Maddox cut in, "Did Elmore see the shooter?"

"I don't know," Cash said. "He hasn't regained consciousness."

"I'll ride with him in the ambulance," Maddox said.

"No, I will." Jasper squared his shoulders. "He trusts me."

Cash exchanged a wary look with Maddox, but Maddox agreed.

"The kidnapper escaped with the money," Cash said.

Despair nagged at him.

The ransom was paid—but still, no news of Tyler.

FEAR SEIZED BJ as the ambulance drove away.

Was Tyler with the kidnapper? If so, why wouldn't he have left the little boy? Because he'd never intended to return him to his grandfather?

The reasons that came to mind terrified her.

She and Cash drove toward the hospital in silence. Maddox was close behind.

By the time they parked at the emergency entrance, the medical staff was rushing Elmore to surgery. Maddox met them in the waiting room.

"Did he wake up?" BJ asked.

"No." Maddox looked grim-faced.

"What did you find out about Frannie Cooper's murder?" Cash asked.

"Not much. The sheriff who investigated gave me a copy of the notes he took during his interviews, but I haven't had time to go through them."

Jasper stalked toward Maddox, his jaw tight with anger. "I want to talk to you, McCullen."

Maddox gave a quick nod. "Of course. How about getting us some coffee?"

"I'm not your errand boy," Jasper snarled.

"I know that," Maddox said. "But we may be here a while. I have to call my deputy, then we'll talk. I'll meet you in the cafeteria."

Jasper stomped away and headed toward the cafeteria.

"You have your hands full, Maddox. Let me look at those files while you deal with Jasper," BJ said.

Maddox shrugged. "I guess it won't hurt."

Maddox hurried to his vehicle and returned a few minutes later with a file. "Let me know if you see anything." Then he headed down the hall to meet Jasper.

BJ carried the file to the seating area in the waiting room. Cash walked down the hall and returned with two cups of coffee. She handed him half the notes and she took the remainder.

"Frannie's mother was an alcoholic who hadn't spoken to her daughter in years," BJ said as she skimmed the notes. "She was in and out of rehab, graduated to cocaine and overdosed the year after Frannie was murdered."

"Sounds like Frannie had a rough life," Cash muttered.

BJ nodded. "Frannie lived in an apartment. According to her neighbors, she loved Drew and did her best to take care of him, but on a waitress's salary she couldn't make ends meet. When Drew became ill, she missed so many days of work the owner fired her."

Sympathy for Frannie engulfed BJ.

"Frannie found another job working the late shift at a brew pub, but one night she was shot in the alley behind the bar. The owner found her the next morning. Police determined the killer was probably a drunken customer, but never made an arrest."

"No security cameras?" Cash asked.

"Apparently they weren't working."

Cash cursed. "Dammit, BJ. Look at this." He angled a paper with a list of people interviewed.

BJ's heart raced when she zeroed in on a familiar name.

Sheriff Jim Jasper.

CASH'S HEAD REELED. "Jasper was in the bar the night Frannie died."

"Seems too coincidental," BJ said.

"Damn right it does." Cash rifled through the notes to the interview with Jasper. "Says here that he was looking for a stolen car, and traced it to the bar."

BJ worried her bottom lip with her teeth, and glanced down the hall where Jasper had disappeared. "Did he know Frannie?"

"Said that she just waited on him."

Cash's mind raced. "Other than Tyler and Drew

sharing the same father, Jasper is the only common factor between Frannie and Sondra."

BJ made a low sound in her throat. "Cash, what if Jasper fathered the boys?"

Cash's stomach knotted. He'd never liked Jasper. "I guess it's possible. Since Sondra's father and Jasper were friends, she probably thought it would cause trouble if Elmore knew they'd been together, especially if Jasper had taken advantage of her." The pieces began to fit in Cash's mind. "Jasper would also know how to frame me."

BJ drummed her fingers on the table. "That's true. He would also have access to criminals, someone he could have paid to drug you, kill Sondra and pose as you for that camera. Someone like Taft or Spillman."

"We have to let Maddox know," Cash said.

"Right now all we have is a theory," BJ said. "We can't accuse a sheriff of murder or kidnapping without more evidence."

She was right. Jasper would make Maddox's life hell if they made accusations.

"Let's talk to Jasper's deputy," BJ said. "Maybe he knows more about Jasper."

Going out on their own without telling Maddox was chancy. But Maddox had stood up for him. He didn't want to jeopardize Maddox's career—or his life.

BJ looked up as Maddox approached. "Did you find anything?" Maddox asked.

"Nothing concrete," BJ said. "Where's Jasper?"

"He insists on waiting here for Elmore to wake up. I'm going to do the same."

BJ handed Maddox the files. "All right. Let us know when he regains consciousness."

Cash followed BJ outside, feeling antsy. Jasper had been quick to arrest him.

Because he'd made the perfect patsy?

He was all alone. A man with no money and no way to defend himself. A man who was close to Sondra, and who Elmore thought was Tyler's father.

Jasper had also been friends with Elmore, so Elmore hadn't once suspected that his friend would betray him.

BJ DIDN'T LIKE where this case was going. But the elaborate way Cash had been framed was orchestrated by someone who knew what he was doing.

Dark clouds rolled in, a light rain drizzling down as they drove toward Jasper's office.

If Jasper was Tyler's father, he wouldn't have wanted Elmore to know—why? Because he didn't love Sondra? Because he didn't want a child?

Because he had forced himself on Sondra and knew Elmore would kill him if he found out?

A deputy's vehicle sat in front of the building. She climbed from the truck, and they walked up the sidewalk together. In spite of his bad memories, Cash opened the door and strode in, shoulders squared.

She followed, her stomach clenching. If Jasper was as devious and coldhearted as she suspected, he had covered his own butt.

So why ask for a ransom? To make it appear that the kidnapping and Sondra's murder was about money?

The deputy looked up at her with a scowl as she

entered, his frown deepening when Cash halted in front of him and crossed his arms.

"What the hell are you doing here?" the deputy asked.

BJ adopted a poker face. What if the deputy knew what Jasper had done and was covering for him?

ANGER COILED INSIDE CASH. He stepped forward, tempted to jerk a knot in the deputy's collar, but BJ placed a warning hand on his arm and he froze.

He had to keep his cool or he'd wind up locked up again.

"I have some questions," BJ said "Did you know Sondra Elmore?"

The young man shook his head. "I never met her, but her father and Jasper's father were friends."

"What about a woman named Frannie Cooper?" BJ asked.

"Can't say as I do. But I've only lived here three months. Moved here from Cheyenne."

"Did Jasper ever mention having a child?" Cash asked.

BJ shot Cash a dark look. The deputy's brows rose in a puzzled expression. "Where'd you get that idea? Jasper doesn't have any family. Heard him say he liked it that way. He was planning to run for Mayor and didn't want anything to get in the way."

An election could mean that someone might expose his secrets.

Having two illegitimate children, abandoning one who was sick, and possibly assault or rape charges against him would definitely have tainted his chances.

Sounded like a motive.

Cash glanced at the sheriff's desk. He'd like to take a look inside. Not that Jasper would be foolish enough to leave any evidence behind.

Except for the evidence he'd planted against Cash.

BJ thanked the deputy for his help, then they stepped outside. "It's time we let Maddox know what we learned."

Cash removed his phone from his pocket. "I'll call him." He punched Maddox's number and filled him in.

"Good god, that makes sense now," Maddox said. "Jasper's been behind everything."

"Is he still there?" Cash asked.

"He left a minute ago. Said he had a clue he was going to check out, but he refused to tell me what it was."

"He may be going to Tyler," Cash said. "Did Elmore wake up?"

"Not yet." Maddox muttered a sound of frustration. "I'll call Jasper's office and see if he's there."

"We're there now and the deputy hasn't seen him."

"Then I'll check his house," Maddox said. "You and BJ sit tight. I'll keep you posted."

Cash didn't like it, but he had to trust Maddox. Hard to do, but so far he'd been aboveboard with him.

He ended the call, then he and BJ walked over to the diner to get coffee. From there, they could see the sheriff's office and would know if he came back.

Thirty minutes passed with no news from Maddox. Jasper didn't show either.

"I can't stand this waiting," BJ said. "I'm going to talk to the deputy again."

Cash stood. "All right."

"Wait here, Cash," BJ said. "He might tell me more if I'm alone."

Cash exhaled. "Okay, but I'll be right outside the door if you need me."

They walked across the street and BJ went inside. Cash paced the sidewalk, every second increasing his anxiety as he waited.

Finally she came out, but she looked anxious. "Jasper owns a cabin in a desolate wooded area. He likes to go there and think sometimes."

Cash's heart pounded. "He might have Tyler there."

"That's what I was thinking."

Cash's keys jangled as they hurried to his truck.

"I'll call Maddox," BJ said.

Cash nodded, and she made the call while he

entered the address the deputy had given her into his GPS.

BJ must have gotten Maddox's machine because she left a message.

He fought the fear eating at him as he drove. Twenty minutes later, they were in the wilderness when BJ's phone buzzed. Maddox.

She put him on the speaker.

"I got your message," Maddox said. "You may be right. Jasper isn't at his house so he may be at that cabin."

"We're on our way there now," BJ said.

"Dammit, I warned you two to let me handle this," Maddox said.

"I'm sorry, Maddox," Cash said. "BJ tried to reach you."

"Just wait on me when you get there. Jasper is dangerous," Maddox said.

"We know that," Cash said. But Tyler was worth it.

"Devon phoned about Sondra's computer," Maddox continued. "Jasper is Tyler's father. Sondra found out Jasper had another son, Drew, and started asking questions about his mother. One of Jasper's emails warned her to keep quiet or else."

Maddox hung up, and Cash accelerated as they crossed the rugged terrain. If Jasper was desperate, he might be planning an escape.

Cash clenched the steering wheel in a white-knuckled grip and veered down the graveled road. The truck rumbled over dirt and potholes, across rugged land that was untamed and so far off the grid a person could hide out for months.

Suddenly a burst of light illuminated the sky above, streaking the dark clouds.

"Oh, my God," BJ cried. "That's a fire."

Terror clawed at Cash, and he pressed the accelerator. Tyler...

# *Chapter Twenty-Two*

Flames burst into the sky, lighting the dark clouds and sending panic through Cash. He rounded a curve, spotted a barn on fire and screeched to a stop.

"Tyler might be in there!" He vaulted from the truck "Call for help!"

Just as he neared the barn, Jasper ran out. Cash jerked him by the collar. Jasper raised his weapon at Cash, but Cash was fast, and knocked it from his grasp. The gun flew into the dirt a few feet away.

"Let me go, you son of a bitch!" Jasper yelled.

Cash slammed Jasper against the barn wall.

Heat from the fire seared him. "You killed Sondra and took Tyler. Is he in that barn?"

Jasper's eyes flashed with rage. "She was going to ruin me!"

Cash squeezed the man's neck. "*Is* Tyler in there?"

Jasper slammed his fist into Cash's stomach. Cash grunted and threw the man to the ground, then punched him in the chest. Anger heated his blood, and he punched him again.

"Let him go, Cash," BJ said in a commanding tone.

She inched toward them, her hands gripping Jasper's gun. She aimed it at Jasper.

"Go get Tyler, Cash!" she shouted. "If he moves, I'll shoot him."

Cash dragged the sheriff to the wooden railing of the pen, grabbed the man's handcuffs and cuffed him to it. Then he turned and ran toward the burning barn.

Fire crackled and popped. Wood splintered. Flames danced from the rear of the barn and crawled along the straw on the floor. The fire hadn't yet reached the front door, but it was creeping toward it.

"Tyler, are you in here?"

Heat seared Cash's neck. A board from the roof splintered off and fell at his feet. He jumped over it, dodging fire as it crept up the wall.

"Tyler!" He weaved past two stalls, then made it to the last one. Tyler was hunched in a corner, tied to a post.

Rage fueled Cash's adrenaline. Flames were eating the wood, catching the straw near the little boy's feet. Tyler had been gagged, but he was trying to scream, and pulling at the ropes.

Cash ran to the tack room, grabbed one of the horse blankets, then darted back toward Tyler. The poor little boy's eyes were panicked and tears streaked his dirty cheeks. Smoke clogged the air.

Cash beat at the flames as he ran through them. He used his pocketknife to cut the ropes, wrapped the blanket around the little boy, then picked him up. Tyler sagged against him, trembling with fear.

Cash covered Tyler's head and body with the blanket, then ran through the barn. The front was just catching fire. He ducked his head against Tyler and hurried outside.

Flames licked at his arms and legs, but he beat them away with one hand, then carried Tyler to a tree several hundred feet away.

BJ was still standing guard over Jasper, who was growling and cursing.

She glanced over her shoulder at Cash and relief filled her face when she saw Tyler.

Sirens wailed in the distance. Maddox roared onto the scene along with an ambulance.

Tyler coughed, but clung to Cash. Cash rocked him back and forth until the medics reached them.

BJ DARED JASPER to make a move. She'd never shot a person before, but this coldhearted bastard had left an innocent little child in a barn to burn to death.

"How could you kill your own son?" BJ asked.

Jasper's harsh face hardened even more. "I didn't ask for a kid."

"You know how it happens and you didn't prevent it," BJ said, furious. "Even worse, you have two children, neither of which you've taken responsibility for."

"He's your son," Cash snapped. "How could you hurt him?"

"That's your fault," Jasper said. "If you two hadn't kept snooping around, I would have taken the money and gotten him back to Elmore. But you had to interfere."

BJ tightened her fingers around the gun. Poor little Tyler was crying in Cash's arms.

The big tough man's body was shaking as well, as if he was overcome with emotions. He was so tender with Tyler. He'd saved his life.

The medics knelt beside Cash and Tyler and began to examine Tyler.

Maddox approached slowly. "BJ, I've got it. You can put the gun down."

Her hand jerked, but Maddox gently pushed the weapon down with one hand. "I've got it, BJ. He's not going anywhere."

BJ released the breath she'd been holding and lowered the gun.

The next few hours passed in a blur as the medics transported Tyler to the hospital for observation. Cash rode with him, and she drove his truck. Whitefeather arrived to meet the crime team, with promises they would have all the evidence they'd need to put Jasper away for a long time.

Maddox was transferring him to jail to book him.

While Cash stayed with Tyler and they settled him into a room, BJ checked on Drew. Candace, his social worker, was sitting by the little guy's bed.

"How's he doing?" BJ asked.

A sad expression tugged at the woman's mouth. "Not very well, I'm afraid. We need a donor soon."

"We found his father." BJ's mind raced with the beginnings of a plan. "He needs to be tested to see if he's a match, right?"

"Right. Will he agree to it?"

BJ removed her phone from her purse. "I'll make sure he does."

She dropped a kiss on the sleeping little boy's head, then stepped into the hall to make a call.

CASH COULDN'T RELAX until he knew Tyler was all right.

But how could he be all right when his mother had been murdered and his father had tried to kill him?

How did a child overcome that kind of trauma?

He hadn't known his own parents, but at least they had wanted him. Neither one of them had tied him up in a burning building and left him to die.

Instead they'd died trying to find him and his brother. Maddox had filled him in when they were in the waiting room. The killer made it look like his mother crashed her car while she was drinking, but the accident hadn't been an accident at all. She'd been drugged.

And his father, Joe McCullen, had been poisoned.

The doctor who examined Tyler motioned for Cash to step into the hall.

"Is he going to be all right?" Cash asked.

"Physically, he's fine. But emotionally, he may have a hard time. Are you family?"

No, but he wished he was. He explained about Jasper and Sondra's murder. "His grandfather, Lester Elmore, was brought in suffering from gunshot wounds."

The doctor scratched his chin. "We're required to confer with Children and Family Services. Depending on his grandfather's condition, Tyler may be placed in foster care."

Cash fought a reaction. So many bad memories for him. He didn't want Tyler to suffer the way he had.

And what would happen to Tyler's half brother, Drew?

"If Tyler wakes, tell the nurse to assure him I'll be back."

He rode the elevator to Elmore's floor and stopped at the nurse's station. "I was with the ambulance that brought Lester Elmore's grandson in. How is Mr. Elmore?"

"He's in and out of consciousness. It's still touch and go."

"Can I see him?"

Maybe Tyler could stay with him until Elmore

was released and feeling better. Would Elmore consider taking in Drew?

"Are you family?" the nurse asked.

Cash hesitated. "Not technically, but I'm close to his grandson. You know he was kidnapped?"

"Yes, I saw the story on the news. I've been praying for the little boy," the nurse said.

"Elmore was shot trying to pay that ransom," Cash said. "It might help him to know that we rescued Tyler and that he's safe."

"Of course it would." She led him to Elmore's room. "Just don't stay too long or upset him. He needs to rest."

Cash nodded. He had bad blood with Elmore. It was possible that his presence might agitate the man.

But...he needed to know that Tyler was safe.

That he had to fight to live.

Because Tyler needed his grandfather now more than ever.

BJ CLENCHED HER phone as she explained the situation with Jasper to her father.

"So Cash Koker is a McCullen?" her father asked.

"Yes, Dad, and he's innocent."

"Hmm." A pregnant pause. "I'm sure the McCullens are happy."

"They will be," BJ said. "Right now we're dealing with Sheriff Jasper."

"He's guilty. You've got the proof. He'll go to jail."

"Yes, but it's complicated. He had another son, a little boy named Drew, who needs a kidney transplant badly. Jasper may be a match, but he hasn't agreed to testing. I was thinking that if we had leverage, maybe offered him a deal, he might agree to donate his kidney."

"If he killed two women, kidnapped his son for ransom and tried to kill him, then he should rot in jail."

"I agree," BJ said. Jasper had admitted that Drew's mother had threatened to expose him if he didn't pay her. "But Drew may not make it without that transplant. Can you talk to the DA and ask him to take the death penalty off the table in exchange for a kidney? That is, if Jasper is a positive match to Drew."

Another hesitation. "I'll make the call."

BJ closed her eyes and said a silent prayer that her plan would work. Once Drew was healthy, it would be much easier for him to find a forever home.

She phoned Maddox and relayed her conversation with her father. Maddox agreed to coerce Jasper into taking the tests.

BJ went to check on Tyler and Cash. Maybe if Drew got well, he and Tyler could connect. Then neither little boy would have to be alone again.

Of course, that depended on Elmore...

CASH EASED INTO a chair beside Elmore. The astute man who'd made his life hell looked frail in the hospital bed, not so imposing.

Cash took a deep breath, determined to forget his animosity toward the older man. Nothing mattered now except Tyler.

"Mr. Elmore, it's Cash Koker," he said in a low

voice. "I don't know if you can hear me, but Tyler is safe." He hesitated, waiting for a reaction.

Elmore's eyes fluttered open and he struggled to focus. He licked his lips and tried to make his voice work, but coughed instead.

Cash spotted the water on the tray, inserted a straw and pressed it to the man's lips. Elmore took a sip, his eyes fluttering again.

"Did you hear me, Elmore? Tyler is safe and alive."

"Thank God." Elmore groaned and slowly turned his head to face Cash. "Jasper?"

"Maddox—Sheriff McCullen—arrested him. He's going to prison."

"Did he hurt Tyler?" The question came out a croak.

"He's shaken up, but he'll be all right."

Regret racked Elmore's face. "I've wasted so much time with Sondra and Tyler."

Cash's throat thickened. "It's not too late for Tyler."

The man's lip quivered. "Thank you for…saving him."

"He needs you," Cash said. "You're all he has."

Elmore shook his head, then tried to lift his hand. "Tyler loves you."

Cash took the man's trembling hand in his. "I'll be around if he needs me. That is, if...you want."

Elmore nodded. "If I don't make it, promise me you'll take care of him."

Cash clenched his teeth. "You are going to make it, Mr. Elmore. You can't leave Tyler now."

For a weak man, his grip on Cash's hand grew stronger. "Promise me," Elmore said, his voice cracking.

Cash swallowed hard. "I promise."

A small smile tilted the corners of Elmore's mouth. Then he closed his eyes and drifted back to sleep.

Cash stood, dumbfounded. What the hell had just happened?

Had Elmore really asked him to take Tyler if something happened to him?

Suddenly, the heart monitor beeped and machines trilled. A nurse rushed in and waved him away from the bed. “Get a crash cart!” she shouted to another nurse.

Cash was pushed to the side while a team tried to revive Elmore. Several minutes passed.

But Elmore didn’t respond.

Instead, he slipped into death.

## *Chapter Twenty-Three*

Cash stared at the scene in the hospital room in shock.

A few minutes ago Elmore had asked him to take care of Tyler if something happened to him.

Now Elmore was dead.

"Cash?" BJ's voice barely registered through his dazed state. "What happened?"

"He's dead," Cash said in a gruff voice.

Her hand brushed his back. "My God, poor little Tyler. What's he going to do?"

Cash pivoted, heart aching. "I don't know. Elmore actually asked me to take care of him, but...I can't."

BJ's expression softened. "You could, Cash. Tyler loves you."

Cash shrugged. "I have nothing to offer the kid. No money. No home. I don't even have a damn job." He ran a hand over his rough, beard-stubbled jaw. "Besides, the law would never give him to me. I'm not blood kin."

Sympathy registered in her eyes. "I'm sorry. I…we'll talk to the social worker." She guided him away from the sight of Elmore lying dead in the bed.

They walked down the hall toward Tyler's room. "I spoke with Maddox about Drew and Jasper," BJ said. "He's going to pressure Jasper to be tested for the kidney transplant."

Anger threatened to make Cash explode. No man should have to be bribed to step up for his own kids. "You think he'll do it?"

"I put a call in to talk to the DA about a deal to take death row off the table if he cooperates."

A rock and a hard place. Jasper deserved to die. But Drew needed that kidney.

"How's Tyler?" BJ asked.

"Physically, he'll be fine." Cash pushed open the door and they both stepped inside. The little boy was curled on his side, deep in sleep. He looked peaceful—but his life had been anything but peaceful lately.

His mama and grandfather were dead, and he was alone in the world.

"I'll call Candace," BJ said. "She's sitting with Drew. Maybe she can help."

Admiration for BJ flooded Cash, and he took her hand in his. "I don't know how to thank you for everything you've done, BJ. I…you're amazing."

Her eyes sparkled, the attraction simmering between them bursting to life. "So are you, Cash. So are you."

BJ'S LUNGS SQUEEZED for air.

She wanted to say so much more to Cash. But the hospital wasn't the place.

Maybe when the legal issues were settled, when they returned to Horseshoe Creek, they could talk.

Although she wanted more than talk…

A nurse walked by, jarring her back to reality and the job she had to do.

Had Elmore told anyone other than Cash his wishes? If not, it would be difficult to prove that he'd actually asked Cash to raise the little boy.

Candace met her in the hallway outside Tyler's room. "Tyler's grandfather just died." She explained about Cash's conversation with Elmore.

"Unfortunately, we'll have to see what Sondra and her father stipulated in their wills," Candace said. "Until then, Tyler will be placed in a temporary foster home."

"He's already been through so much," BJ said, her heart aching. "Staying with strangers will only add to his trauma."

"I'll make arrangements to handle his case myself." Candace squeezed BJ's hand. "Try not to worry."

BJ went to join Cash while Candace made the phone call. Cash sat by Tyler's bed, his head bowed.

BJ remained still, giving him space and time,

until he finally glanced back at her. He looked so tortured that she crossed the room to him and rubbed his back.

"Candace is going to help us, Cash."

She realized she'd said *us* and knew she'd lost her heart to Cash and the little boy.

Candace's heels clicked on the floor as she entered. "My supervisor agreed to let me handle Tyler's situation."

She joined them by Tyler's bed. "Mr. Koker, BJ explained what happened. I'll do everything I can to help you."

"Thanks. I appreciate that." He patted Tyler's hand. "I hate to see him suffer any more."

Candace offered him a smile. "You obviously love him. Both of you look wrung out. Why don't you go home, shower and get some rest? I'll stay here with Tyler in case he wakes up."

Cash looked torn. "I don't want to leave him."

"Who knows if he's slept at all these last couple of days?" She smiled softly. "You need to rest, too."

Cash hesitated again, but finally stood. "All

right. I guess I do smell like smoke and could use a shower. Call me if he wakes up."

Candace promised she would.

BJ and Cash left the hospital together and drove in silence back to Horseshoe Creek.

Exhaustion lined his features as he parked at the cabin.

BJ wanted to console him, to assure him that everything would work out. But how could she do that?

Legally, he had no right to Tyler, not if Elmore hadn't specified it in his will.

He slid from the truck, walked around and opened her door. He made no invitation for her to join him at his cabin, and she reminded herself that he had a lot on his mind. That he was worn-out and needed a shower and sleep.

So she walked up the path to her cabin and watched him drive across the way to the one where he was staying.

It was best she not give in to her desires.

Sleeping with him would only complicate things.

He'd already stolen a piece of her heart. She needed to keep the remainder intact. If not, she wouldn't survive when they parted.

And now the case was over, she'd have to go back to her job and her life.

Besides, Cash had a new family. And she wasn't part of it.

CASH'S ARM ACHED like the devil from that flesh wound, smoke permeated his clothes and hair, and he felt as if his arms had been singed.

It didn't matter, though. Tyler was alive.

But that kid faced a tough road, losing his family in a violent way.

He'd probably have nightmares about the fire.

Did he even know that Jasper was the man who'd fathered him?

God, Cash hoped not. What would that realization do to a little kid?

Probably screw him up for life.

Tyler needed someone to love him, to help him through the grief he'd feel over his mother's loss.

Cash shucked his clothes and stepped under the warm water, then dunked his head. He quickly lathered and washed off, although when he closed his eyes, memories of BJ's sweet touch made his body ache.

Last night she'd kissed him. Not just kissed him, but really *kissed* him, like she wanted more. Like she wanted to be with him.

Like she enjoyed his hands touching her.

He wanted them on her now. Wanted to feel her delicate skin beneath his work-roughened fingers. To feel those gorgeous legs wrapped around him. To inhale her feminine scent and taste her, and slide his naked skin against hers.

His erection swelled to a throbbing need, and he turned the water to cold to tamp down his libido.

It didn't help.

Wanting her wasn't just about his body's hunger. Somewhere along the way he'd fallen for her soft heart and her stubbornness and her desire to help others. She'd defended him, and she would fight for Tyler and for his brother, Drew.

The world needed more people like her.

*He* needed her.

The thought sucker punched him.

He'd cared about Sondra, but as friends. He'd never wanted to be friends and lovers before.

He wanted both with BJ.

He dried off, yanked on clean jeans and a shirt and stared at the empty bed.

Rational thought fled. He didn't want to be alone.

He pivoted and headed outside. Only one way to find out if BJ wanted him, too.

The light was burning in her cabin. In the bedroom.

He walked across the grassy area, then hurried up the path to her door. One knock, and she opened it, her face a beautiful sight.

She'd showered and changed into pajama pants and a thin white camisole. No bra.

Her plump breasts pushed against the fabric, her nipples stiff peaks.

"BJ?"

Her eyes lit with desire, then she curled one

hand around his head and pressed her lips to his. "I was hoping you'd come," she whispered against his cheek.

Her softly spoken words and the passion in her kiss ignited his hunger, and he pushed her backward into the room.

Her arms wound around his neck, her hands urgent as she raked her fingers through his hair.

He cupped her butt with one hand, pressing her against his thighs as he deepened the kiss.

Hunger ignited, raw and primal. He dragged his mouth from hers and planted frenzied kisses down her neck. She tasted like sweetness and hope and salvation, everything a man like him needed but didn't deserve.

He started to pull away.

But she cupped his face in her hands, looked into his eyes with need, and he forgot his reservations.

He needed her. And dammit, she wanted him, at least for the moment.

That would do for now.

BJ HAD NEVER craved a man's touch the way she craved Cash's. The emotional connection from working the case and finally saving Tyler intensified her desires.

His body was hard, his muscles thick from hard work, yet his hands gentle as he traced one finger down her jaw. She sucked in a sharp breath, his earlier hesitancy only fueling her growing feelings for him.

Cash was honorable. A man who fought for what was right. A man who'd saved a little boy's life.

A man who would protect a woman, as well.

She parted her lips and tasted the salty skin of his neck as he trailed his fingers over her breasts through the thin tank top. Her nipples beaded to stiff peaks, yearning for more.

She urged him closer with sweet whispers, and stroked his back down to his muscular backside, reveling in the pleasure in his moan.

"BJ?" he whispered against her ear.

She took his hand and guided him to the bedroom. He paused, raking his eyes over her with appreciation, stirring erotic sensations inside her. A come-hither smile curved her mouth.

There was no turning back now.

She was going to give herself to Cash Koker.

The pleasure would be worth whatever the price of her heartbreak when he left.

# *Chapter Twenty-Four*

Cash wanted BJ naked. Skin to skin.

Bodies moving together.

He planted kisses along her jaw and neck, tasting sweetness and desire as he lifted the tank top over her head.

Her breasts spilled out, sending his erection straining against his jeans. Her nipples were rosy and stiff, begging for a man's touch.

He cupped her breasts in his hands, then lowered his mouth and sucked one taut bud into his mouth. She threw her head back and groaned, arousing him even more.

Her fingers tunneled through his hair as he laved one breast, then the other, and she pulled him toward the bed. He gently shoved her onto the quilt, but resisted when she reached for him.

Instead, he focused on her pajama pants. They were some kind of flimsy material and felt soft to his hands, but not as soft and satiny as her bare skin.

She wasn't wearing panties.

His breath caught at the blatant hunger in her eyes. She urged him closer, her whispered sigh a plea for more. But he didn't want to rush this.

He threaded his fingers in her hair, tilted her neck back and kissed the sensitive skin behind her ear. "Tell me what BJ stands for," he murmured.

She moaned his name.

He drove his tongue inside her ear and stroked one nipple between his fingers. "Tell me, BJ."

A soft sigh escaped from her, and she rubbed his back. "You'll laugh."

"No, I won't," he said, as he kissed her again. "I want to say your name when I'm inside you."

BJ shivered, shifting so she rubbed his thick length against her belly. "It's Brandy Jane," she murmured.

A smile tugged at his mouth as he looked into her eyes. "Brandy Alexander?"

She nodded, heat in her gaze. "My mother's favorite drink."

He chuckled and she slapped him playfully. "I told you you'd laugh."

He brushed her hair back and kissed her again, this time fervently. "I want you, Brandy Jane."

She tugged at his jeans. "I want you, too, Cash."

Instead of mounting her, he lowered himself to the floor, then spread her legs with his hands.

She whispered his name, her body trembling as he placed his tongue at her sweet center. He drove his mouth over her sensitive spot, teasing her with his tongue and savoring her honeyed taste.

She reached for his arms, silently urging him to enter her, but he held back. More than anything he wanted to give her pleasure, to make her feel special. Wanted.

To be the person she needed and deserved.

He shut out the doubts. He'd have time for those later.

He lifted her hips slightly, then closed his lips over her center, adding his finger to the madness to tease her. Her hips bucked and she trembled.

Her sigh of pleasure ended with a long groan and she came apart in his arms.

His need became more urgent, and he stripped off his clothes, braced himself above her and pressed his rigid length between her legs.

Rational sense intruded for a millisecond, long enough for him to roll on a condom.

Moaning his name, she clutched his hips as if she couldn't wait, then rubbed herself against his erection. She felt like heaven.

It would be hell to leave her when it was over.

But they both needed tonight.

He stroked her dampness with his throbbing sex, until his release burned inside him, begging for escape.

Murmuring how much he wanted her, he stroked her sex with his. The first touch of her body quivering and clenching around him nearly made him shout.

He thrust inside her, filling her to the core,

then drove himself in and out, teasing her until the urgency swept them both away.

Erotic sensations pummeled him as he came inside her.

She clawed his back with her hands as she joined him on the ride.

BJ SNUGGLED UP to Cash's chest and closed her eyes, the euphoria of making love with him triggering emotions that threatened to overflow.

She was in love with the man.

But she couldn't confess her feelings. He would think she was crazy and desperate. Besides, he didn't need his lawyer latching on to him like a lovesick teenager.

Hadn't she vowed not to get involved with another client? Her father had insisted on professionalism. She'd failed him once.

He'd never allowed her to forget it, either.

Cash slid from the bed and padded to the bathroom, and she instantly missed him. Was he going to leave and retreat to his cabin?

Her heart fluttered. He should leave.

But he returned, crawled in beside her and drew her to him again.

She curled against him and fell into a deep, exhausted sleep.

Hours later, the nightmares of her son's death woke her. Aaron's voice cried out, "Help me, Mommy. Save me."

Grief and anguish bombarded her, and she sobbed his name. She could see his little hand reaching out for her to pull him from the water. Hear him choking for a breath as his head bobbed up and down.

She screamed his name, but suddenly his face faded into the fog and little Drew's pale face appeared. Drew was so sick.

He needed help. Needed that kidney.

Tears blinded her and she jerked upright.

Cash sat up quickly and rubbed her arm. "BJ?"

"I couldn't save him," she cried. "I wanted to but I couldn't."

Cash made a low sound in his throat, then rubbed her back in small circles and pulled her into his arms. She closed her eyes, the pain as relentless as it had been the day she'd lost him.

That pain would never go away.

A hollow emptiness robbed her of breath, the same void she'd lived with for two years now.

"I'm sorry, BJ." Cash pressed a kiss to her hair. "So sorry."

She fought the urge to scream that he couldn't possibly understand.

No one could.

CASH DIDN'T KNOW what to do. One minute, BJ had been sleeping in his arms, content and purring his name.

The next she'd been screaming her son's.

Anger and frustration at her situation ripped through him. He had no idea how to help her.

"I'm sorry," BJ whispered through her tears.

"You have recurring nightmares?"

She nodded, then pulled on her robe. "I need to be alone, Cash. Please go."

He chewed the inside of his cheek, then stood

and rubbed her arms. "Let me help you, BJ. Come back to bed—"

"No," she said sharply. "I can't, not when I see my dead son every time I close my eyes. When it was my fault he died."

A muscle jumped in Cash's cheek. "BJ, it wasn't your fault. You know that." Didn't she?

"It was. I knew my ex had a drinking problem. But I never thought he'd drink and drive, not with Aaron in the car."

"Had he done that before?"

"No, never." Her voice broke. "He loved Aaron and was always good with him."

"Then you couldn't have known, BJ," Cash said quietly. "Some things are just out of our control."

BJ swiped angrily at her tears. "Please, Cash, just go. I need to be alone."

Cash went still, his heart pounding. He'd thought they'd had a connection when they'd made love. That she might even…care about him.

But she'd simply needed comfort.

He didn't regret giving it to her.

He was a fool, though, for thinking that a relationship with her could be anything but temporary.

She had her demons to slay. And he had his own.

Tyler's face flashed in his mind. Tyler needed a parent. Someone who'd understand him.

He'd probably need therapy.

Self-doubts ate at Cash.

Even if the court granted him custody of Sondra's little boy, what did he know about being a father?

"Cash, please be gone when I come out." She hurried into the bathroom and closed the door with a resounding thud.

He yanked on his jeans.

Damn. He should be grateful she wasn't making demands, talking about the next time they'd see each other, wanting to be his girlfriend.

He'd never had a real girlfriend.

But something about her made him want to claim her as his.

Still, she wanted him gone. She was probably

already regretting sleeping with him. After all, her father was a powerful attorney.

They were from different worlds.

And he had to accept it.

THE NEXT TWO days BJ worked to wrangle in the ridiculous feelings she had for Cash. She'd met with her father again. He was proud of her for helping solve the case.

He'd also been inquisitive about the McCullens, but she hadn't let on that she'd fallen for Cash.

Disgust made her sigh as she let herself back into her old apartment. The situation had drawn them together—that was simply all this attraction was.

The deafening quiet as she stepped into the entryway struck her.

The place seemed cold. Empty.

Lonely.

Just as she was.

She had been ever since she'd lost her son.

She remembered the smile on Drew's face

when she'd dropped by the hospital, and her heart melted. Drew would survive.

But he had no place to go when he was released, except to another foster home.

She'd gotten the charges against Cash completely dropped. He was a free man—free to do whatever he wanted and make a life with whomever he wanted.

She made several calls to Elmore's attorney about Tyler's custody issue. Shockingly, the man had called a meeting with Cash and the McCullens to discuss the situation.

Jasper had confessed to murder and kidnapping, and accepted the DA's deal. The tests proved he was a match for Drew. They'd performed the surgery that night. Thankfully, Drew's body had accepted the match and he was recovering.

Rain pounded the roof outside and slashed the windowpanes. She dragged her rolling suitcase to her bedroom, the pristine white walls and comforter stark and almost depressing, just like the dark storm clouds outside.

She'd thrown away all the color in her life when Aaron had died, because he loved colors.

One of the many rainbow drawings she'd kept and framed still sat on her dresser, a reminder of him and the energy he'd had in life.

She went to the desk and removed the folder of his sketches. More rainbows, the sun shining, happy faces and horses. She'd promised to sign him up for horseback riding lessons, but she'd never gotten the chance.

Tears filled her eyes. A million years ago, she'd had rainbows and laughter and a little boy's precious voice and smile in her house for a while.

Drew's face haunted her. Had he dreamed of rainbows or a future at all? Or had he just been waiting to die?

Sorrow for Aaron swelled inside her. She couldn't bring her son back or help him now.

But that other little boy needed love. A family. A mother. Someone to take care of him.

She grabbed her keys, jogged outside, then drove to the Memorial Gardens center where she'd laid Aaron to rest. Emotions pummeled her as she parked and crossed the grassy gardens to a tiny spot in a section marked Little Angels.

Padding softly to his tombstone, she knelt and ran her finger over the marker.

"I love you, buddy, I always will," she whispered. Then she began to tell him about Drew.

"You will always be my son, and you own my heart." She kissed her fingers, then pressed them on the plaque where his name was etched. "What would you think if I let this other little boy live with me? He doesn't have a mommy or anyone else." Except for Tyler, and they were still working out the details to see if Cash gained custody of the boy.

The wind ruffled the trees. A breeze tossed leaves around the grave.

Suddenly, a rainbow appeared, the brilliant colors shimmering across the stone marker and grass.

A seed of joy and hope burst inside her. She kissed her fingers again and laid them on the stone.

The rainbow was her answer, her wise and

wonderful son's way of telling her that it was okay for her to love another child.

She stood, antsy to call the social worker.

# *Chapter Twenty-Five*

*Two days later*

Cash's stomach tightened as he entered the lawyer's office. Conan Cambridge, Elmore's attorney, greeted him with a handshake. Maddox also shook the man's hand.

Having Maddox here meant more than Cash would ever have thought. When he'd relayed Elmore's last words to him, Maddox had insisted on accompanying him.

BJ was waiting inside, her hair tugged back in a bun, the professional mask in place. She wore a jacket and skirt, as if she thought dressing in a business suit would dull his desire for her.

But nothing could do that.

He wanted to strip the damn suit and make her writhe beneath him again, naked, hot and sweaty.

The thought disturbed him to the core.

"Have a seat, Mr. Koker," Cambridge said. "I've been talking with your lawyer, Miss Alexander."

BJ gave him a stiff smile, one that ticked him off, because she was acting like she didn't know him, as if he'd never been inside her and heard her cry his name in the throes of passion.

Cash and Maddox claimed the wing chairs across from BJ, who was perched on the leather love seat.

"We're here to discuss Mr. Elmore's wishes for his grandson, and his will," Cambridge said.

Cash chewed the inside of his cheek, his heart pounding.

"Miss Alexander informed me of your conversation with Mr. Elmore when he was on his deathbed," Cambridge said.

Here it was. That fancy lawyer would say it

wasn't valid. No one else had heard it. Cash had made it up.

A muscle ticked in Cambridge's jaw. "Unfortunately, Elmore died without changing his will."

Cash shifted and started to say something, but BJ shook her head, indicating for him to hold his tongue.

"That said, I can tell you that Elmore left his estate to his daughter, Sondra, and her son, Tyler. I've reviewed Sondra's will, and surprisingly, she made stipulations that in the event of her death, she wanted you to raise Tyler, Mr. Koker."

Shock stole Cash's words. "She did?"

He nodded. "She also stipulated that she wanted Tyler to be with you, but she wanted her father to have access to the boy." He paused. "She wanted them to have a relationship."

The lawyer's words reverberated in Cash's ears. "What does this mean?"

Cambridge pulled at his tie. "It means that if you're agreeable, Tyler Elmore will be placed in your custody." A serious frown carved lines in the man's weathered face. "Of course, a social worker will be assigned to make home visits, check on the child's well-being and confirm that you are able to care for the boy."

Cash's head reeled in shock, but he nodded.

"One more thing, Mr. Koker," Cambridge said. "Lester phoned me the day you tried to make the ransom drop and were injured. He told me he'd been wrong about you."

Cash couldn't believe this was happening.

"According to his will, Tyler inherited Elmore's ranch," Cambridge continued. "You being his guardian, you and Tyler can live on his ranch."

"I don't think Elmore would like that," Cash said.

Cambridge crossed his hands on his desk. "You risked your life to save Tyler, Mr. Koker. Lester knew that. He told me he was going to offer you a job as his head foreman. With Lester gone and Tyler a minor, someone will have to take over."

The man paused. "How do you feel about all this?"

Cash pinched the bridge of his nose, emotions

flooding him. Love. Relief. Worry. He'd never had a father. He didn't know if he could handle the job.

"You do want custody of Tyler, don't you, Cash?" BJ asked softly.

Cash's gaze met hers. "Yes."

The lawyer stepped outside the door for a moment, and more self-doubt pummeled Cash. He leaned close to BJ and spoke in a conspiratorial whisper. "But what do I know about being a father? What if I mess up?"

BJ squeezed his hand. "You love him. That's what he needs most." The McCullens were good people and would help their newfound brother raise the boy.

The social worker Cash had met at the hospital with Drew entered the room, Tyler's tiny hand tucked in hers.

The little boy looked up at him with worry and sadness, melting Cash's heart as he knelt before him. "Tyler?"

Tyler's lower lip quivered. "They said Mommy's gone."

"I'm sorry, bud." Cash wiped a tear from Tyler's cheek. "But you've got me."

"The lady said I can live with you, Cash," he said in a small voice.

"That's true." Cash's heart pounded. "I'd like that, Tyler. What do you think?"

Tyler nodded, then threw himself against Cash's chest. Cash wrapped his arms around the little boy, Tyler's tears mingling with his own. He might not know how to be a father. He might mess up.

But he'd do the best he could. And from now on, Tyler would be his son.

"ARE YOU SURE you want to do this, BJ?"

BJ squared her shoulders and faced her father. She wanted his blessing, but she didn't need it. She had to follow her heart. "I've never been so sure of anything in my life."

His stern face softened. "I understand. I know the last two years have been rough."

"They have," she admitted. "I made mistakes, Dad. My judgment wasn't always good."

"Everyone makes mistakes, honey," he said in an uncharacteristically thick voice. "You need to forgive yourself and move on."

BJ blinked, surprised at his comment. "I wanted to make you proud, Dad."

He left the chair behind his desk, walked over to her and captured her hands in his. "I am proud of you, sweetheart. I realize I haven't always shown it, and we disagreed sometimes. I didn't know how to help you after you lost Aaron." His voice warbled. "I…hated seeing you hurting, and didn't know what to do to make it right for you."

"You couldn't make it right," BJ said, her heart splintering at the sound of pain and helplessness in his voice. "No one could. I had to grieve. And…I still am grieving."

"I've grieved, too, baby. But you deserve to go on." He lifted her hands and kissed them. "All I want is for you to be happy, honey."

BJ inhaled a deep breath. "Giving Drew a home will make me happy."

He nodded, understanding softening his eyes.

"Take all the time off you want. If you need anything, money—"

"Thanks, Dad, but I don't need money. I have savings," BJ said. "Once Drew's settled, I may come back, even if it's only part-time."

"You always have a place here." He hugged her, and BJ kissed his cheek. She hadn't expected him to take her news so well. Maybe in her grief and guilt, she'd been too hard on him.

Her phone buzzed. Candace. She connected the call.

"BJ, I have good news. You can take Drew home today."

Her heart fluttered with joy and relief. She would never hold her son again. But Drew needed her and a home, and she could give him that.

*Five days later*

CASH STOOD OUTSIDE the McCullen farmhouse, still in awe of the new family he'd found. They were having a barbecue celebration tonight in his honor. Mama Mary had cooked a feast of side dishes, while the McCullen men grilled steaks and burgers. The wives and kids gathered in the yard, talking and laughing, warmth exuding from them all.

Tyler didn't want to go back to the guesthouse or to Elmore's. Neither did Cash.

He would never feel at home there. So they were staying at Horseshoe Creek in the cabin. His brothers—it still felt weird to refer to them as that—planned to help him build a house of his own on the land.

Mama Mary had embraced him and Tyler, welcoming them into the family as if they'd always been around. Tyler followed Brett's son around like a puppy, and Sam had taken him in like a kid brother, showing him the ropes.

His brothers had given him a box of letters and cards their mother had written to him after his disappearance. She hadn't forgotten a single birthday or holiday and poured out her love, and her determination to find him and his twin.

He'd cried like a baby when he'd read them.

Cash made arrangements for Elmore's head

foreman, a robust, friendly man named Wayne, to run the ranch. Maddox, Brett and Ray had heard good things about the ranch hand, whom they knew from the Cattleman's Club.

Mama Mary seemed taken with him, as well. According to Rose, she'd invited him to supper several times the past few months.

Tonight Roan Whitefeather and his wife, Megan, joined in the barbecue celebration.

The McCullens had had their problems, but they remained family and supported each other through thick and thin.

Cash wanted Tyler to grow up here.

"What are you going to do about BJ?" Maddox asked.

Cash tilted his hat against the waning sun as he watched Tyler toss a horseshoe. Brett and his little boy had quickly drawn Tyler into the game.

"What do you mean? I'll have to make payments on what I owe—"

"Her fee was taken care of," Maddox said. "I meant, what are you going to do personally?"

Cash gave him a dark look. He'd never told

Maddox how he felt about BJ. Hadn't told anyone. "I was just a case to her," he said quietly.

Maddox grunted. "You weren't just a case, at least not toward the end. I saw the way the two of you looked at each other."

He shrugged. "You must have misunderstood."

"No, I didn't," Maddox said, his gaze straying to his wife, who was rocking their baby in the rocking chair on the porch. "Let me tell you something, little brother. Real love only comes along once."

His chest squeezed. "Maybe. But I've got Tyler now and nothing to offer a woman like her."

"That's BS," Maddox said. "You have part of our spread, and she adores Tyler."

Cash couldn't argue with that. But something else was bothering him. "I've been thinking about Drew. He's Tyler's half brother. I think the boys should be together, but I don't know if I can manage two kids and work a ranch."

"Mama Mary would be happy to watch the boys," Maddox said. "She made a great mama for me and Brett and Ray."

"I don't doubt that," Cash said, affection for the woman warming his heart.

The trouble was, he wanted BJ to be with them, too.

But she'd asked him to leave her alone.

Maddox patted Cash's back. "Don't be afraid to go after what you want."

Cash straightened. Was that his problem?

All his life he'd thought his mother and father hadn't wanted him. That no one had.

But he'd found the McCullens, and they'd embraced him with love and support.

Was it possible that BJ might want him, too?

BJ SETTLED DREW into bed. He was still recovering from the surgery and needed rest, but he was gaining strength every day. He'd seen Aaron's rainbow drawings and had wanted to paint one himself.

Now both boys' art hung on the walls.

She tucked the covers around him. "I'll be in the next room." She brushed his hair from his forehead. His eyelids were already heavy, drooping. He reminded her of her son. Yet he was different, his own little man. "Call me if you need anything, sweetie."

His eyes widened for a second. "Where am I going after here?"

BJ smiled. The poor little boy was so insecure. "You're not going anywhere, Drew. I want you to live with me. Forever."

"Forever?" he said in a tiny voice.

"Yes, sweetie." She planted a kiss on his forehead. "That is, if you want. I'll be your mommy."

"But what if you get tired of me?" he asked, big-eyed.

BJ pulled him into her arms and rubbed his back. "I'll never get tired of you, Drew. Never."

His little body trembled, but he sniffed and relaxed against her. She rocked him back and forth until his breathing evened and he fell asleep.

BJ gently tucked the blanket around him, and guided her son's stuffed lion into Drew's arms. The lion had given Aaron comfort when he woke in the night. It had given her comfort, too, during the last two years.

Now it was doing the same for Drew.

She could almost see Aaron smiling, running in the yard, playing hide and seek, then curling with the lion at night as she read him a story.

Odd, how, since the accident, she'd remembered only the anguish of losing her son. Although her heart longed for him, and it felt bittersweet, she was finally able to remember the happy moments. To see him smiling, not crying out for her to save him from death. She'd even dreamed the night before that he was holding his father's hand and they were walking together in heaven.

She planted another kiss on Drew's forehead, then tiptoed from the room.

It would take time, patience and love for Drew to heal and accept that he had a permanent home.

His insecurities reminded her of Cash's childhood. Never having love or the comfort of a secure home.

Cash would give security to Tyler, though.

Maybe at some point, once she overcame her heartbreak over not being with him, they could get the boys together. Tyler and Drew both deserved to know they had a brother.

She showered and poured herself a glass of wine, then sank onto the sofa in her den. Tomorrow she'd start searching for a small house, someplace with a yard and trees to climb and acreage to run and play. Some place homey like the cabin where she'd stayed on Horseshoe Creek…

Her doorbell dinged, and she tensed. Ever since Candace had called with the news that she could keep Drew, she'd been afraid that something would happen and the courts would reverse the decision.

She took a deep breath and hurried to the door. Shock hit her when she saw Cash standing in the doorway, his expression strained.

Something was wrong.

"Did something happen with Tyler?"

He shook his head. "No, he's good. He's with Brett's boy. They've become fast friends. And Mama Mary is smothering him with love and food, just like he's a McCullen."

BJ couldn't help but smile at the reminder of

the sweet, robust woman with the bigger-than-life heart. "She is special. Everyone ought to have a Mama Mary in their life."

Cash murmured agreement, then shifted as if he was suddenly uncomfortable. "The McCullens have all been great."

BJ smiled. "I'm glad, Cash. You deserve a family."

His gaze darkened. "It still feels weird. Like they might change their mind any day."

She understood that feeling. She was afraid of losing Drew. "I think you can count on them."

Cash sucked in a deep breath. "I want Tyler to feel that way about me."

The fear tinging his voice struck a chord.

She motioned for him to come in. "I'm glad you stopped by. I…wanted to talk to you."

He stepped into the entryway. "You did?"

She nodded. She wanted to tell him she loved him, but held her tongue. "I talked to Candace about Drew."

His eyes widened. "I was going to do that. I thought he should live with me and Tyler."

Her chest clenched. Was that the reason he was here? Because he wanted to take Drew away from her?

## *Chapter Twenty-Six*

Cash hadn't meant to start out by talking about Drew, but if he and BJ had a chance, she had to accept him for the man he was, baggage included. No pretenses.

"How did you know Drew was here?" BJ asked.

Cash stared at BJ in surprise. "Drew is here?"

She nodded. "Did you talk to the social worker?"

"Not yet." He'd wanted to talk to her first. "What's going on?"

"I have temporary custody of Drew."

Cash was shocked. "You do?"

"Yes, I want to adopt him." She folded her arms across her chest. "Is that why you're here? To tell me you're going to fight me for him?"

"God, no," Cash said. Her raised brow reeked of suspicion, a reminder that she had trust issues. "I just wanted to see you."

Her expression softened as she ran a hand through her hair. The movement drew his gaze to the fact that it was still damp. She wore pajama pants and a tank, too, just as she had the night they'd made love. This tank was more modest, built with one of those bras inside it, but her cleavage spilled over, making his mouth water.

He wanted her again.

A blush stained her cheeks, as if she'd read his mind. "Then what are you doing here, Cash?"

A smile tugged at his mouth. The desire in her eyes gave him hope and courage. "I…miss you," he said gruffly.

She bit her lip, her expression wary. "If you came for a booty call, that's not going to happen. Not with Drew here."

"I'm not here for a booty call," he said gruffly. "I want more than that."

BJ's eyes narrowed, but she took a step toward him. "What do you mean, Cash?"

A rush of hunger shot through him, and he closed the distance between them. The scent of her feminine body wash suffused his senses, making him crazy. "I want you, BJ."

"Cash—"

"Let me finish. Yes, I want to sleep with you, but I want to sleep with you every night."

"Ahh, Cash," she said in a soft whisper.

Her hair lay in long waves around her shoulders, and he reached out and tucked one silky strand behind her ear. "For a long time, I didn't think I deserved to have someone like you in my life. That no one could love me."

Warmth and tenderness filled her eyes, and she pressed her hand against his jaw. "You're a brave, honorable man, Cash. You deserve the McCullens. And you deserve love."

"I want us to be together. To be a family. Forever."

"If this is about Drew—"

"It's not about Drew, although he and Tyler will be part of this." Cash traced a finger over her lips. "It's about you and me, BJ. I love you,

Brandy Jane Alexander. I…want to build a life with you."

Yearning glowed in BJ's eyes, and she wrapped her arms around his neck. "I love you, too, Cash."

Then she tilted her head and fused her mouth with his. He yanked her to him, hungry and aching for her touch.

But most of all for her answer.

The kiss was erotic, teasing, promising more. But he needed the words.

"BJ?" he whispered. "Will you marry me?"

A sexy smile brightened her eyes, and she kissed him again, then whispered, "Yes."

Cash picked her up and swung her around. He'd gone from being locked in a cell, accused of murder, from feeling all alone, to finding a bride and two kids.

Except for his missing twin, life was perfect. He had brothers and their families and Mama Mary.

And now he'd have a family of his own.

* * * * *